"You won't do. Can't use you."

Sara stared at him in amazement. "Dr. Williams, you haven't even asked about my qualifications. Don't you care about those?"

"No. Goodbye, Ms.—whatever you said your name was. Don't waste any more of my time."

The unreasonable Joshua Williams was surpassing even his own reputation. "Listen," Sara argued, "you've never even seen me before today, so I don't know what you could possibly have against me."

"You're too damn pretty! That's the last thing I need. Another pretty, muffin-brained snit of a girl. Get the idea now?"

For a moment she was speechless. Then she got to her feet and said briskly, "My name's Bennett. Sara Bennett. And you don't really have any choice. Unless you can actually prove I'm a 'muffin-brained snit' you're stuck with me. That's the way things work."

Ellen James has wanted a writing career ever since she won a national short-story contest when she was in high school. *Growing Attraction* is her sixth Harlequin Romance novel. She and her husband, both writers, love to travel. They also share an interest in wildlife photography and American history.

Books by Ellen James

HARLEQUIN ROMANCE
3052—HOME FOR LOVE
3069—THE TURQUOISE HEART
3118—TWO AGAINST LOVE
3154—LOVE'S HARBOR
3202—LOVE YOUR ENEMY

GROWING
ATTRACTION
Ellen James

Harlequin Books

TORONTO • NEW YORK • LONDON
AMSTERDAM • PARIS • SYDNEY • HAMBURG
STOCKHOLM • ATHENS • TOKYO • MILAN
MADRID • WARSAW • BUDAPEST • AUCKLAND

ISBN 0-373-03254-4

Harlequin Romance first edition March 1993

GROWING ATTRACTION

CHAPTER ONE

"ANYBODY HERE?" Sara edged her way through the greenhouse door, peering over the stack of books she was carrying. No answer came to her question and at first she thought the place was deserted. Then she saw a pair of legs poking out from behind a table of ferns and ficus. The legs were in kneeling position and appeared to be quite strong and rugged—very masculine, indeed. They were clothed in navy corduroy jeans, with feet clad in running shoes. These were scuffed shoes, obviously well used, nothing frivolous about them. Well, Sara could approve of that. In the year and a half since she'd taken over her father's farm, she'd learned to whittle every bit of frivolity from her life. Her own feet were clad in high-top buckaroo boots, plenty of service left in them in spite of their worn and battered leather.

Sara maneuvered a path among tables of leaf cuttings, potting benches and bags of peat. The air was heavy and warm, scented with the green perfume of a hundred growing things. She breathed in deeply; she loved the smell of plants and fresh soil. She stopped to address the corduroy legs.

"Excuse me...Dr. Williams, is that you?"

The legs moved restlessly, as if displeased at this interruption. "Yes, yes, it's me. Be with you in a min-

ute," came a gruff voice from behind the table. The
curt tone immediately put Sara on her guard. She'd
already heard several dismaying stories about famed
botanist Dr. Joshua Williams. He was rumored to be
cantankerous, demanding, unreasonable—impossible to work for in any capacity. Yet everyone here at
Colorado's Glenn State Agricultural College also said
that Joshua Williams was a brilliant teacher and that
the school was lucky to have such a renowned scientist on its faculty. He was a world authority on hybrid
corn. After listening to all the stories, Sara had simply decided she'd wait to meet Dr. Williams in person
before passing her own judgment on the man. No
matter what, she was going to be spending a lot of time
around him. At the moment she was certainly becoming well-acquainted with his legs.

Goodness, he was wearing one red sock and one
green sock. Was this some new fashion? Sara shifted
the books she was carrying to her other arm. She
leaned down and tried to look under the table to see
the rest of Joshua Williams, but her view was blocked
by a veritable jungle of angel's trumpet, bougainvil-
lea and horsetail rushes. Sara moved forward, craning her neck to see around the table. Now she could
gaze unobstructed at the almighty Joshua Williams—
at the back part of him, anyway. He was a big man,
the breadth of his shoulders emphasized by a bright
red-and-green-and-blue plaid shirt. At least the shirt
matched both of his socks. His hair was rumpled and
untidy, a russet so vivid in color it made Sara think of
ripe winter apples and of sugar maples turning fiery
red in the fall.

He was busy potting seedlings of some sort as he knelt there on the floor and he seemed to have forgotten completely about Sara's presence. She cleared her throat.

"Dr. Williams, I—"

"In a minute, I tell you. Don't bust your begonias."

Sara raised her eyebrows. Joshua Williams was a colorful man, with a colorful way of speaking. But she was beginning to grow impatient. She rocked back and forth on the heels of her boots, clutching her stack of books. She didn't have any time to waste. Juggling the farm work along with her studies was proving to be a monumental task and she was trying frantically to stay on top of things. This morning she'd been up before dawn. She'd milked the goats, run some mineral blocks to the cows in the south pasture and spent several hours working on the combine—changing the wear plates and oil filters and hydraulic fluid, hosing off the radiators. When she'd finally glanced at her watch she'd realized she was already late for her first class at the agricultural college. She'd made a mad dash into town in her rattly old pickup, attended three classes in a row, then careered straight across campus to the greenhouse. She hadn't eaten lunch, the goats were waiting to be milked again, she still needed to clean the sieves on the combine and she had to start clearing a field for the winter wheat that would be her thesis project this semester. Meanwhile, this Williams fellow was telling her not to bust her begonias!

"Dr. Williams, if we could just get things started—"

All she heard from him this time was a noise rather like "harrumph!" He sounded like her old pickup when the choke was stuck. And he went right on potting his seedlings, paying no attention to Sara.

She'd had enough of standing there. She set her books on the floor with a smack, her long braid of acorn brown hair swinging over her shoulder. Then she marched around the table and knelt down beside Joshua Williams. She scooped up one of the scraggly seedlings and began nestling it into a pot of bedding soil. This was the strangest little plant, with a skinny stem that wobbled under the weight of one spidery leaf. Sara could name just about any plant by sight, but for the life of her she didn't know what this was. A distant cousin of the philodendron, perhaps?

Poking her fingers into moist, rich soil was beginning to soothe away her irritation and impatience. She tweaked the little plant's leaf. "There," she murmured to it. "Whoever you are, you'll do fine. Dig your roots in deep. And remember, think nitrogen."

Sara sensed she had Joshua Williams's attention now. She turned toward him, ready to be businesslike. And yet, looking into his gray eyes, she couldn't say a thing—businesslike or otherwise. She ought to have been prepared for this first glimpse of his face. The many rumors about him had invariably included a footnote about how handsome he was. But learning this fact for herself was startling.

He wasn't conventionally handsome. His features were brash and definite—his nose substantial, his mouth wide. The total effect was rough-hewn, as if an exuberant sculptor had begun to mold Joshua's face but had then forgotten to smooth out the edges. So it wasn't any pleasing arrangement of features that contributed to Joshua's appeal. It was the vibrancy, the life that radiated from him even when he remained motionless. She found herself grinning foolishly at him.

Joshua Williams, however, didn't grin back. He scowled at her, his unruly eyebrows drawing together. "Who the devil are you?" he demanded. "And why the heck are you mauling my plants?"

"I'm Sara Bennett, your new research assistant. And I didn't maul anything—"

"Research assistant? *You?*" He made it sound as if she'd just proclaimed herself president of the United States. She flushed while he gave her a thorough and obviously disapproving perusal. Why, the man was inspecting her as if she had root rot or mealy bugs. She didn't appreciate it, not one bit. She tried to gaze back at him steadily, but it wasn't easy. Self-consciously she adjusted the brim of her seed cap, wishing she could hide the freckles on her nose. She wondered if her eyes looked blurry from lack of sleep. Usually her eyes were her best feature, a clear hazel just as her father's had been. But she knew that too many nights of falling into bed after midnight—only to tumble out again before dawn—were beginning to take their toll on her. She probably looked a wreck ... wisps of hair coming undone from her braid, her shirt wrinkled because she couldn't spare a minute to iron. The worst of it was that she cared what Joshua Williams thought of her. But why did she care? So far he'd been nothing but rude and obnoxious.

"You won't do at all," he said. "You're not what I asked for. Go back and tell them to get it right next time."

Sara clenched her hands, feeling the potting soil underneath her fingernails. "You act like I'm a shipment of defective mulberries or something. But believe me, Dr. Williams, I'm the right person for this job. The most qualified. That's why the Dean of Plant Sciences hired me." Sara didn't mention that she was also desperate for this job. The stipend was the highest of any assistantship on campus. With it she'd receive a tuition waiver and actually have enough cash to repair her forty-year-old tractor—as well as keep herself and the dairy goats in feed until the end of the semester. Whether or not she had time for the job was immaterial. Somehow she had to hold everything in her life together. Just a few more months... she'd make it through the harvest and she'd graduate from college at last. With any luck, she'd be home free after that.

Joshua was shaking his head emphatically. "Can't use you. Go back to the dean and tell him to send somebody else."

Sara's temper was fraying like a strained piece of rope. "Dr. Williams, you haven't even asked about my qualifications. Don't you care about those?"

He potted another seedling. His hands were large yet deft, all his movements precise. He pressed an odd sort of thermometer into the soil, then recorded a measurement in the notebook open beside him.

"Goodbye, Ms.—whatever you said your name was. Don't waste any more of my time."

She sat back on her heels, amazed at his unreasonable behavior. He was surpassing even his own reputation.

"Listen, I don't know what your problem is," she said. "You've never seen me before today, probably never even heard my name—you can't remember it from one minute to the next, that's for sure. So I don't know what you could possibly have against me—"

"You're too damn pretty, all right? That's the last thing I need. Another pretty, muffin-brained snit of a girl waltzing in here who doesn't know a geranium from a giraffe. Get the idea now?"

For a minute she couldn't say anything. Then she scrambled to her feet. "Aphelandra," she rapped out, pointing at a plant with big, white-veined leaves. "Also known as zebra plant. And that shrub over there is a shrimp plant. That's a flamingo flower, that's a bird of paradise . . . and there's a dragon plant and a cockscomb. I'd say you just about have the entire animal kingdom covered. Except for a giraffe, of course." She picked up the seedling she'd potted, watching its long, spindly stem wobble back and forth. "Now, this little guy looks like a giraffe to me. What do you think?"

He gave her a sour look. "Your wit overwhelms me, Ms. . . ."

"Bennett. Sara Bennett." She set the pot down. "Dr. Williams, you don't really have any choice. I *have* been assigned as your research assistant. Unless you can actually prove I'm a 'muffin-brained snit,' you're stuck with me. That's the way things work."

He seemed extremely disgruntled by now. "Give me the thingamajig," he demanded.

"What are you talking about?"

"Lord, just hand it over. The thingamabob you research assistants always bring with you from the employment office. You know what I'm talking about. That blasted yellow form I'm supposed to sign about twenty million times after I've read it."

"It appears I'm not the one who has muffins for brains," Sara grumbled under her breath.

"What did you say?" He gave her a suspicious glance. She didn't answer, fishing the yellow form from the back pocket of her jeans. It was all crumpled up and had bits of linseed meal clinging to it, but Sara handed it over with a flourish.

Joshua shook a few oats away from the form. "What did you do, try eating this thing for dinner?"

"As a matter of fact, the goats almost did eat it. They like the taste of yellow paper. Not that I can blame them. I'm sure it's much more delicious than plain old white . . ." Her voice trailed off at his acid expression. "Anyway," she continued forcefully, "go ahead and read it. You'll see I'm the person for this job."

He leaned back against a leg of the table and read the form in frowning silence. He seemed unaware of the fern fronds dangling down to brush the top of his head. After a moment he stirred. "Not a bad grade point average," he admitted. "But it says here you dropped out of school over a year ago—only one semester away from graduation. Why was that?"

Her shoulders stiffened. "My father died," she said reluctantly. "I had to take over the farm right away or it would've gone under." She tried for a noncommittal tone, but it wasn't any use. Her emotions always hovered near the surface and she couldn't deny them now, especially when she was talking about a subject that meant so much to her. "Actually, I wanted to take over the farm. It's been in my family for generations. I loved going to school here, but it wasn't nearly as important as keeping the farm going. I'm glad I made the choice I did."

He rattled the yellow sheet. "So why come back now? Why start plaguing *me?*"

For Pete's sake, he made it sound as if her return to school was a personal vendetta against him. Why did he dislike her so much without even giving her a chance—without knowing her at all? It unsettled her, and it made her angry, too. She frowned at him.

"I only have one semester left. And it's imperative that I graduate. Once I do, I'll qualify for the Farm Managers Program. And then I'll have enough money to run the farm properly." Truth was, the Managers Program was virtually her last chance for keeping the farm. She'd inherited the place along with a staggering amount of debt, machinery that was completely outdated and no hope of credit from any bank in the state of Colorado. She'd dearly loved her father, but he'd been an impractical man who'd taken the farm to the brink of ruin. For months after his death she'd struggled with the financial disaster he'd left to her; last spring she'd barely had enough money for planting.

Then the banker here in Glenn Creek had told her about a private foundation called the Woodrow Donnelly Trust...and its new Farm Managers Program, ready and willing to loan money to help modernize struggling farms just like Sara's. But there was a catch.

She needed a college degree to qualify as a manager under the program. With harvest coming on, there couldn't be a worse time for her to return to school. Yet she couldn't afford to delay, not even for a few months. She'd survive the grueling schedule ahead of her. She *had* to survive it.

Joshua went on reading her employment form intently, as if hoping to find something that would disqualify her for the job.

"Look at my employment history," she urged. "When I was at school before, I worked at the greenhouse. Dr. Lendell gave me an excellent recommendation."

"I'm not Lendell."

"Obviously not." Sara glared at Joshua Williams, silently regretting that wonderful, easygoing Dr. Lendell had retired last year, only to be replaced by this impossible and unreasonable man.

Joshua rattled the form again. "I don't like it," he muttered. "You only came back to school so you could qualify for some damned assistance program. And then they fob you off on me. What kind of dedication are you going to have to this job?"

The last of Sara's weary self-control snapped. "I'll be the most dedicated employee you ever saw! Please quit twiddling around and just sign the darn form so we can get on with it. I tell you, the dean hired me. Even you can't go against that."

Joshua rubbed his jaw, a contemplative expression on his face now. He surprised Sara by taking a pen from his shirt pocket, uncapping it and actually signing the form in three different places. He thrust it at her.

"You forgot to sign over here," she pointed out. "And down there at the bottom."

"Blasted bureaucratic bunk..." He scrawled his bold signature two more times, then rose to stand beside her. He was even taller than Sara had imagined. She herself was tall and sturdy, but next to Joshua Williams she felt...well, almost petite. And feminine, in spite of her wrinkled cowboy shirt and faded work jeans. But she didn't *want* to feel this way. She retreated a few steps from him, trying to regain the proper perspective on herself.

He rested his hands in the back pockets of his corduroys. "So let's get to work. You're right, Ms. Bennett. No sense in 'twiddling around.' First, your duties. You'll be responsible for—"

"Just a minute."

"Lord, we haven't even started and already you're complaining."

"I'm not complaining. But I have to get a notebook so I can write down what you're saying. Your instructions, and all." She went to her books and rummaged among them until she found one of her notepads. Pencil ready, she waited for Joshua to proceed. She wanted to show him from the very beginning that she was conscientious, that she took the job seriously. But he didn't act impressed in the least.

"Your duties," he repeated in an ominous tone. "You'll be assisting me in the conservatory as well as the greenhouse. Doing everything from feeding and watering the plants to raking up dead leaves. And you'll have to know how to lead tour groups. We get lots of young school kids in the conservatory, and you'll have to keep them in line. Stop them from tearing leaves off plants or throwing candy wrappers in the pond. It's not the most exciting job. I've had assistants quit because they think I'm only asking them to do menial work."

Sara jotted some notes, then glanced up. "I used to handle all that for Dr. Lendell. I like anything to do with plants and I'm good at controlling kids."

Joshua almost seemed disappointed by her positive response. "Next. I'm going to expand the horticultural-sciences program. I'll expect you to draft my new class plans...and do any clerical work the department secretaries can't manage. It'll probably be a lot of typing." He paused, looking expectant and just a little pleased.

Sara tightened her fingers on her pencil. She knew exactly what was happening. Joshua Williams was throwing out the classic challenge of college professor to research assistant, asking her to do his typing even though she wasn't his secretary...and wasn't paid to be his secretary in any shape or form. He was doing it on purpose—not because he *wanted* her to do his typing, but because he wanted her to protest and quit. His first tactic to get rid of her hadn't worked, so now he was trying another one.

She stared at him. His eyes were a silver gray, cold and hard. Even though Sara's teeth had clenched, she managed to push out the necessary words.

"I'm a decent typist. Give me access to a computer and I'll be better than decent."

He didn't look pleased any more, and Sara knew she'd won this round. He began pacing back and forth among the African hemp and African violets.

"You'll attend the faculty council meetings and you'll take minutes. Plus, you'll attend all my classes, run the audiovisual equipment and grade exams. Under my supervision you'll coordinate the undergraduate research projects. Of course, you'll assist in my own research. You'll do cleanup in the lab, tabulate results, run errands for supplies. You'll go to the library and abstract journal articles for me...and we're talking lots of journals here. Lots of them." He paused again, but Sara merely continued to jot down notes with furious speed. She was simmering with indignation, though. Dr. Williams was asking her to be a combination teacher's aide/secretary/janitor/gofer. No research assistant she'd ever heard of was required to handle so much work. She knew that, Joshua Williams knew that...and he was waiting for her to storm out of the place. No chance!

"Anything else?" she asked calmly.

He picked up a trowel and tapped it against his palm. "I'm going to need you at least thirty hours a week, maybe more."

He'd finally gotten to her. She almost broke her pencil in two. "Dr. Williams, research assistants only work fifteen hours a week. They *can't* work any more than that. The school doesn't have the funds—"

"I have plenty of grant money I can allocate for an assistant."

"I can't possibly work that many hours! I have the farm, my classes, my own schoolwork to do."

He shrugged, a glint of triumph in his eyes. "If you're not happy, you can go complain to the dean. I'm sure he'll give you another assignment."

She gazed at him steadily. "I wish you'd tell me what it is you have against me. Do I remind you of someone else, is that it?"

He gave a wry grimace. "Unfortunately, something tells me you're unique, Ms. Bennett. One of a kind...no, you don't remind me of anyone."

She waved her notepad in exasperation. "So what *is* it? You're trying to make me quit before I can even prove myself. You took one look at me and made up your mind. It doesn't make any sense!"

"Maybe it doesn't. Why don't we leave it at that? You ask for a transfer and I'll get an assistant I can tolerate."

Sara was totally confused. How could the man decide she was intolerable after less than ten minutes? Maybe the best thing for her would be to walk out of this greenhouse and never come back. She'd get another assistantship...and make a lot less money, at a time when it seemed every penny tilted the scales toward success or failure. Just think of the money she'd make if she actually did work thirty hours a week for Joshua Williams! She might even be able to put a little away in case her fickle combine decided to break down again; that had happened last year and nearly cost her the harvest. But how was she going to fit those thirty hours into a schedule already so overloaded it might collapse at any moment?

Joshua was waiting...waiting for her to walk out the door and leave him in peace. But she couldn't do it. She only had four months to go. She'd never forgive herself if she botched things just because this botanist was such an aggravating and obnoxious person. All she'd ever really wanted to do was farm the land her family had owned and loved for generations. All she'd wanted was the chance to run the farm the way it deserved to be run. No, she wouldn't let the almighty Dr. Williams stand in the way of her dream!

Something else tugged at her, too. An odd, disturbing curiosity to know why he'd worked up such an instant and intense dislike for her. It would be a challenge to find out. And Sara had never turned down a challenge in her life.

She tossed her long braid back over her shoulder. "I can give you thirty hours a week. Not a minute more. But during those thirty hours I *will* be the best darn assistant you've ever had. Seems fair enough to me."

He looked downright disgusted. She knew, sure as anything, that he was searching for some fresh tactic to get rid of her. But it was true that even he couldn't thwart college bureaucracy.

"I'll accept you on probation," he said at last, grudgingly. "That's all. You have a week to prove you're as good a worker as you say you are."

It was apparent that Joshua Williams did not lose a battle gracefully. Sara suspected it was going to be one heck of a week. This red-haired man with his cold silver eyes and unmatched socks had the power to make her life miserable. She knew that without a doubt. But she was a strong person. She was ready.

"You're on, Dr. Williams," she said softly. "You're on."

CHAPTER TWO

EXACTLY ONE WEEK LATER Dr. Joshua Williams strode into the lecture hall of Biology 101, bringing with him a dash of color and a whiff of fresh growing things. Sara watched him covertly as she arranged the slide projector for today's presentation. Joshua was wearing another of his bright plaid shirts and forest green corduroy jeans. He seemed to have a fondness for corduroy. That was one of the many details Sara had noted about him during this hectic trial period.

She still believed he was an impossible, exasperating man. But she was beginning to have a reluctant admiration for him, too. Many professors at the school balked at taking on lower-level courses like Biology 101. But Joshua had actually volunteered to teach this class, showing real concern for undergraduates. Every class he held was jam-packed with students. He was a superb teacher, making subjects like cell function and biochemical reaction and chromosome mapping come vividly to life. Sara couldn't fault him for that, no matter how wretched he'd made this past week for her.

Now he plunked his briefcase onto the podium at the front of the lecture hall and sat down casually on a table. His socks were thus revealed. Aha! One was red, one bright green. All week Sara had been watching his feet to see if she'd catch another glimpse of mismatched socks. Today she was finally rewarded. She was more intrigued than ever. Did he deliberately mix up his socks on Fridays? Or was it a haphazard thing with him? Goodness, surely it wasn't an accident. No one could put on one red sock and one green sock and not notice the difference. But he seemed oblivious to the fact.

"Are you ready to begin, Ms. Bennett?" he asked in a dry voice. She started, jerking her head up from this intimate examination of his hosiery. She noticed with chagrin that most of the female students in the class were ogling Joshua, too. It was humiliating that she couldn't control her own fascination with the man, behaving no better than a silly freshman or sophomore. She gave him a brisk nod and clicked to the first slide. One of the students closed the window blinds; at least now Sara could struggle with her disturbing thoughts in the semidarkness.

She listened as Joshua talked enthusiastically about DNA. "Lord, look how beautiful this stuff is," he said. He gestured at the slide screen where a brilliant chain of DNA was illuminated like so many red, blue, green and yellow beads strung into a fanciful necklace. "Today we're going to talk about the components of this incredible structure—the nucleotides. We'll learn about deoxyribose, pyrimidines and purines. Find me a poem any more lyrical than that . . ."

Sara had to grin. He really believed that biology *was* poetry. She clicked to a new slide, this one a convoluted diagram of the DNA coil. Whenever she'd looked at diagrams like this before, she'd felt her own brain was becoming hopelessly coiled. But Joshua somehow made the subject appear simple...logical and, yes, lyrical. He sounded so happy when he said certain words: "Thymine—cytosine—adenine—guanine." Why couldn't he be this cheerful outside the classroom?

Sara had done everything she could think of to establish a good working relationship. She'd been unfailingly punctual, followed all his instructions to the letter, done extra tasks without being asked. She'd even maintained cordiality during an entire week of having Joshua growl at her like an ill-tempered moose. Yet he'd never once admitted she was a decent worker. He treated her with a distant contempt, as if she were something that needed to be sprayed for greenfly.

Now she listened to the inflections of Joshua's voice and clicked to a new slide at precisely the right moment. It was ironic what a good team they made. And it was also ironic that Sara had spent such an unusual amount of time these past few days on her clothes and hair, trying to look pretty for Joshua Williams. It was an alarming compulsion she couldn't seem to resist. This morning, for example, instead of changing the spark plugs on her truck, she'd hauled out her squeaky ironing board and carefully pressed her denim skirt. She hadn't been able to stop there. Next she'd attacked her blue-striped Victorian blouse and her twill riding vest. She hadn't done that much pressing in years; her old iron had almost gone up in steam.

Afterward she'd pinned her mother's cameo brooch at the collar of her blouse, polished her boots to a high gloss and combed her hair out from its braid, allowing it to ripple all the way down her back. Then she'd driven to school, her poor truck coughing and sputtering—still in need of a tune-up. And what good had it done her? None! Joshua reserved all his enthusiasm for DNA and genotypes and phenotypes. Why did she even try to impress him? That first day he'd said she was *too* pretty. Talk about a backhanded compliment. Obviously she wasn't going to snare his attention by getting all gussied up like this. Darn it, why did she want his attention at all? Why—

"Ms. Bennett, could we please see the next slide?" Joshua's polite and rigid voice cut into the swirl of her thoughts. She punched the button on the projector. Oh, yes, he did know how to be polite to her when necessary. He never snarled at her in a public place like the classroom. She almost wished he would. Maybe then they'd get things right out in the open. Maybe then he'd tell her why he detested her so much!

After class Joshua and Sara walked across campus together to his office. At least, theoretically they walked together. Joshua loped along, swinging his briefcase, barely acknowledging her presence. She had to jog a bit to keep up with him, her knapsack bouncing against her shoulder, the heels of her boots making a satisfying "clack clack" on the flagstone path.

"Beautiful day, isn't it?" she remarked.

"Hmmph."

"I'm glad you agree. There's nothing like Colorado in the early fall. A sunny afternoon, a cool breeze . . . what more could a person want?"

"A little silence might be nice."

Sara refused to be daunted. "Isn't this a great campus?" She made a gesture to include the buildings of rose-colored stone with ivy creeping up their sides, the pathways shaded by pine and maple trees. "It's a small, friendly college. You came here from a big university, didn't you?"

No answer. Joshua quickened his pace until Sara really had to jog. She'd noticed that he never talked about himself; he was an intensely private person. It drove her crazy. She'd grown up in a family where she was expected to work hard, but where all emotions were allowed free reign. Even though both her parents were gone, she had the legacy of their laughter and spontaneous joy. She couldn't imagine being as taciturn as Joshua Williams. It made her want to give him a shake, see what was going on underneath his thatch of russet hair.

"So, Dr. Williams, where *are* you from? Originally, I mean. Did you grow up back east somewhere? New England, I'll bet."

He glanced at her with a pained expression. "Why this sudden interest, Ms. Bennett?"

"Hey, I'm just making conversation. It's the kind of thing people do, you know. Small talk and all that. In case you hadn't noticed."

He grumbled something under his breath she couldn't quite catch; it sounded like "cockamamy research assistants." But now and then Joshua could surprise her. He went on to answer her question. "I grew up in San Francisco. I have two sisters who do a nightclub act together. My father's a pharmacist, my mother teaches violin. Is that enough small talk for you?" He didn't wait for a response, just barreled down the path, nodding to a few students who greeted him shyly. Sara brought up the rear like an unwanted caboose. She thought over the tidbits of information he'd tossed to her. Now she could picture him with an entire family. She hadn't been able to do that before; she'd almost imagined him springing full grown from a patch of peat moss.

"Dr. Williams," she said, sprinting to catch up to him.

"What the devil is it now?"

"I wondered what sort of nightclub act your sisters have."

"They dress up in flapper costumes and sing 'Yes, We Have No Bananas,' plus every single damn song from the Marx Brothers' movies. Anything else you have to know? Spit it out now so we can be done with it."

"I'm not *that* interested in hearing about you."

"Fine. Glad to hear it."

Sara really didn't understand. The man had two flapper sisters who sounded absolutely delightful—yet he exuded all the warmth of a sap-sucking leafhopper. Well, it just went to show. The science of genetics was truly a mystery, no matter how much a person might know about DNA.

Sara and Joshua entered the biology building, one of the oldest on campus. Sara loved everything about it: the high ceilings with their mysterious shadows, the dark wooden wainscoting, the glass cases full of dried tansy and yarrow and barley grass. She even liked the musty smell that never left the place no matter how much it was scrubbed down with pine cleaners.

She had to admit she was developing a particular fondness for Joshua's office. She went through the door right on his heels, glancing around at the crowded bookshelves, the posters and calendars tacked to any bare spot on the walls, the corkboard bristling with notes and newspaper clippings, the enormous oak desk that took up most of the floor space. Joshua sat down in an ancient swivel chair and swung his feet onto the desk—apparently still oblivious to his one red sock and one green sock. He picked up a chart on Mendelian peas and disappeared behind it.

Sara didn't mind the opportunity to browse a bit on her own. She believed you could tell a lot about a man by what he read. Joshua possessed a great number of books on botany, agriculture and horticulture. But other volumes on his shelves proved more intriguing: several histories of nineteenth-century America, a guide to medieval English gardens, a battered sociology text and all the science-fiction novels of Jules Verne. It seemed Joshua was a man of many interests.

He lowered his chart of peas and scowled at her. "Ms. Bennett, surely I've given you enough work to do. Why don't you get on with it?"

She settled herself down in the chair across from his desk. "You know, I have this theory about the way you've decorated your walls. Want to hear it?"

"Spare me."

"I'll tell you about it," she said. "You have a little of everything in here. For example, that's a darn good reproduction of Toulouse-Lautrec's portrait of the milliner lady. That calendar has a beautiful photograph of Cape Cod. And there's a funny cartoon you tore from the newspaper...anyway, I think you enjoy things besides science—things like art and photography. But you're not sure about admitting you have this unscientific side to your nature. You compromise by hanging up posters and calendars. Plus, the cartoon shows that *somewhere* deep inside you do have a sense of humor.''

"Ms. Bennett, I'll offer you some free advice. Don't give up farming to be a psychologist. Now—please get to work!''

She propped her elbows on his desk, remaining stubbornly where she was. "It's been an entire week. My trial period's over. But you haven't said one word about what kind of job I've been doing.''

"When I have any complaints, I'll tell you. Meanwhile, you can stay on for another week or two. Shouldn't you be feeding some plants?'' He disappeared behind Mendel's peas again.

Sara drummed her fingers on the cluttered desk. She knew it was too much to expect an actual compliment from the man—but, darn it, she'd knocked herself out to do a good job for him. These days she was sleeping even less than usual, keeping herself going on buckets of sassafras tea. Not quite knowing how, she was juggling the farm, school, her dairy goats and this assistantship that would provide her with sorely needed cash. But now she realized she needed more than money from Joshua Williams. She needed his approval.

She hated feeling this way. Never had a man affected her so contrarily. Was it because she'd got out of practice dealing with men? She hadn't dated once in the eighteen months since she'd taken over the farm. She simply hadn't had the time or the energy to spare for a social life. And yet, before that, she'd been quite outgoing. She'd even been involved in a serious relationship with Ben Timmond, a fellow student. When she'd broken off with Ben, it had been reluctantly. He'd been a steady, dependable fellow, but unwilling to express his emotions. Perhaps the solitude Sara had known since Ben *had* affected her a little. Why else did her heart start thumping like a grain thresher every time she saw Joshua Williams?

At last Joshua smacked his chart down. "Dammit, Sara, will you stop pounding your fingers on my desk?"

She'd been engaged in only the lightest tapping, but she obligingly folded her arms and leaned back. "You called me by my first name."

"No, I didn't."

"Yes, you did. You said, 'Dammit, Sara.' That's fine, believe me. I detest being called Ms. Bennett. It's so formal and stiff."

"Ms. Bennett, get to work or you're fired!"

"You can't exactly fire me. First off, you'd have to file a personnel action notice in quadruplicate. And you'd have to come up with an awfully good reason for termination. After that, your request would have to be reviewed by the Employee Services Committee, the Faculty-Staff Liaison Board, the Dean's Advisory Council. And then—"

"I can't believe this bureaucracy," Joshua groaned, running both hands through his already rumpled hair. "Ms. Bennett, what do you want? Why are you harassing me more than usual today?"

She sighed. "It's very simple. All I want is for you to admit I'm a tolerable worker. I'm not asking for fanfare or trumpets. Just an ordinary 'thank you, job well done.'"

"You know what your problem is? You don't just want a simple thank-you from me. You want to turn this job into a social activity. Next thing I know, you'll suggest we exchange family scrapbooks."

"Do you keep a scrapbook? If you do, it could mean you're actually a little bit human, Dr. Williams. But why can't you say it? Why can't you just admit I've done an okay job? It's all part of basic employee-employer relations."

He stared at her, his gray eyes steely. "I already told you. When I have any complaints, I'll let you know. Until then, just do your work and keep your chatter to yourself. This isn't a sorority house we're running here."

Sara glared back at him. It was obvious he planned to win *this* battle. She couldn't understand why there had to be a war at all, but he seemed determined to make it that way. Didn't he realize a little congeniality between people was what made life rewarding? Livable?

"Maybe you only know how to deal with amoebas," she muttered. "Then again, maybe even amoebas enjoy some affability. See you later, Professor." With as much dignity as possible, she pushed back her chair and marched from the office. She did allow herself the pleasure of slamming the door shut after her.

She hurried across the courtyard to the conservatory. She was glad to have the place to herself; this late in the afternoon the doors were closed to visitors. In the small supply room she tied on her work apron, yanking the strings as she fumed about Joshua Williams. He was the most demanding and least grateful person she'd ever met! Forget the fact that he was also the most . . . compelling. She didn't need the aggravation, that was all. Somehow she'd make it through the next few months. Then she'd graduate and she'd be well-rid of the man.

She tucked a trowel, a claw rake and a pair of shears into the big pockets of her apron. Then she filled a watering can at the sink and went out to the main area of the conservatory. Above her rose the graceful arches of the dome, sunlight flooding down through the panes. She was in a tropical garden, a paradise of plants. The very smell of green surrounded her: pungent and heavy and rich. Orchid trees, coconut palms, giant gold hibiscus flowers, banyans and banana plants . . . surely among all this Sara could forget about Joshua Williams for a little while. She'd been thinking about him far too much. Better to concentrate on whisk ferns that needed misting and weeping figs that needed trimming.

But it wasn't any use, trying not to think about Joshua. This conservatory was his now. He'd changed so many things since taking over from Dr. Lendell. He'd made the place his own. In one corner he'd created a display of succulents, the plump water-storing plants. Donkey's tail and rosary vine trailed from hanging baskets. And every cactus imaginable was included: fish-hook, bishop's cap, pincushion, rabbit's ear. Apparently Joshua believed the desert held as much beauty and delight as the jungle. Sara couldn't help but agree with him. She didn't want to admire his work, his way of thinking, but she couldn't seem to do much about it. She *did* admire him, darn it.

Joshua had made other changes in the conservatory, too. Most of all, he'd organized the place. Dr.

Lendell had perpetually forgotten to label the plants and he'd allowed algae to overrun the pond until the water was dark and murky. Now the water was clear as could be, and every sign was neat and orderly, stuck right in front of the plant where it belonged. Sara experienced a perverse temptation to switch all the signs around, labeling the lipstick tree as a sugar cane, the pepper vine as a breadfruit. Would that finally get Joshua's attention?

She knelt before her favorite plant, a heart of fire. Its long slender leaves burst from the ground, making her think of fireworks splashed in the sky. Gently she ran her fingers over the graceful leaves.

"Some people seem to have hearts of stone," she told the plant. "That's what they want you to believe, anyway. But don't pay attention to them. Being friendly, that's what's important. Sociable, no matter who you're dealing with. Agreeable, good-natured to your employees—"

"Why are you always mauling the plants?" Joshua demanded right behind her. She gasped, straightening up so fast she nearly poked him in the eye with the spout of her watering can.

"Goodness, you scared me half to death," she said. "Don't go sneaking up on me like that."

"I made enough noise to wake a herd of buffalo."

"I think you have that wrong. Shouldn't you say you made as much noise as a herd of buffalo?"

He looked thoroughly out of sorts. "Ms. Bennett. Sara—whatever. Are you willing to hold a conversation with anything? I wonder what's next. You're probably going to tell your life story to some grapefruits and rutabagas."

She flushed, gripping the handle of her watering can a little tighter. The warm, humid atmosphere of the conservatory suddenly felt too intimate; all the greenery crowded around her and Joshua as if to push the two of them closer together.

"It's a fact that plants thrive on pleasant conversation. They like to be touched, too. It soothes them."

He shook his head. "Just what I need. An assistant who's bonkers."

"You're a scientist, aren't you? Scientists all over the world have proven that plants react to feelings and send out their own emotional signals. What about those experiments where they hooked up lie detectors to philodendrons and the plants practically talked back to humans?"

He shrugged. "I'm skeptical about a lot of those experiments. Very skeptical. But even if a plant has a demonstrable energy field capable of manipulation— it doesn't mean you should harass it with useless prattle."

"Plants need human contact. Affectionate contact. Because plants actually feel things. They know when a person's hurt or sad ... they know when someone's trying to hurt *them*." Sara detested that patronizing smile. It was the first time he'd actually smiled at her. But if he was going to be condescending like this, she wished he'd go back to frowning.

"Everything living thrives on emotion," she insisted. "Everything except maybe you, Dr. Williams."

He seemed to be enjoying himself now, folding his arms in a relaxed stance. "So that's what you think of me—I don't have any feelings."

"Oh, you have them, all right. But you'll probably go through the rest of your life repressing them. That's the way Ben was, never could talk about how he felt. It's such a futile way to live."

"Ben? Who's this Ben?" He sounded genuinely interested. Sara liked being gregarious, but for once she decided there was such a thing as saying *too* much. She hadn't meant for Ben Timmond's name to slip out.

"I was only trying to make a point," she said briskly. "You could take a lesson from these plants in here, you really could. That tulip tree, for example, isn't afraid to express a wide variety of emotions and—"

"I get it. Somewhere along the line you had a boyfriend who didn't sweet-talk too well. But what's wrong with that? Never trust a guy who's always spouting off about romance."

Sara took her shears out of her apron pocket and flexed them as if she were about to prune Joshua Williams. "A person can't survive without a little affection. A little feedback, at least. But we were talking about plants. How did we get started on this other stuff?"

"You were complaining about me, and we went on from there."

"Yes, well . . . let's stick to the subject." Sara was beginning to get flustered. It was because of Joshua's proximity on this narrow path. She couldn't think straight and she waved her watering can distractedly. "I suppose you came out here to tell me something or ask me something. You know, about work . . ."

"Yes," he murmured, but he didn't say anything else. He merely gazed at her intently, his eyes more silvery than ever. She gazed back at him, an odd tingling sensation coming over her as if the air had grown too hot and was making her feverish. For some reason she couldn't seem to move away from Joshua, even though she knew that was precisely what she ought to do.

A weighted stillness surrounded them. Sara fancied that the plants were listening to hear what would happen next. She pictured fern fronds curling up like question marks, palm leaves fluttering in anticipation. All this expectancy in the air...surely she wasn't just imagining it. And she gave in to it, simple as that. Instead of stepping away from Joshua, she stepped closer to him. And she lifted her face. Her eyelids drifted downward as she brushed her lips against Joshua's. It was the merest hint of a kiss, but it sent a quiver all through her. She leaned forward a bit, seeking to deepen the kiss. Unfortunately her watering can leaned, too, and she began sprinkling Joshua's feet. They jumped away from each other at the same time, their actions strangely in unison. Joshua's shoes made a squishy sound.

"What in blazes?" he muttered.

Sara was still tingling in that uncomfortable yet enticing fashion, but she managed to look down at his wet feet. Fishing in her apron pocket, she brought out a rag and dangled it hopefully in front of him.

"I must be cursed," he said with a note of complete disgust. "That's it—cursed. Why else is any of this happening? Being kissed by my research assistant! Lord."

Sara began to feel offended. "It was only a little kiss. Not even a kiss, if you think about it. More like a...nudge. An accidental nudge."

"This is all your fault," Joshua accused her. "I don't go around kissing my assistants. Or 'nudging' their lips, either. It's a rule I have, dammit. I just don't do it."

"Now, wait a minute," Sara said indignantly. "It seems to me you were a willing participant. Maybe I started things. But I didn't mean to. I didn't want to do it, that's for sure."

"So why the hell *did* you do it?"

She couldn't very well say the plants had goaded her. He'd accuse her of being cuckoo again. That was how it had felt, though—the rubber plant, the coconut palm and that brazen lipstick tree all encouraging her, egging her on. Damn it, why else had she puckered up for Joshua's kiss? A kiss, by the way, that she hadn't even got to enjoy. The slightest brush of lip against lip...she hadn't been allowed any more than that and yet she was suffering all this grief because of it.

"I tell you, it was an accident," she declared. "An aberration. It won't happen again."

"Hah." He looked her over with even greater disgust than before. "Damn right it won't happen again, Ms. Bennett. You can bet your *begonias* on that!"

CHAPTER THREE

BRRR-RING! Whenever Sara's ancient telephone rang, it sounded like it was having an attack of the chills. Brrr-RING! There it went again, a fitting noise on this cool and gloomy fall evening, rain streaming down the windows. Sara struggled up in a daze from the sofa. She'd dozed off right in the middle of writing a paper on corn production for her agricultural-economics class. Sleep was the last thing she could afford—yet the thing she most craved these days. She resented the darn phone for interrupting this forbidden snatch of rest.

The phone went on shivering: Brrr-RING!

"I'm coming, I'm coming," Sara said grumpily. She padded across the living room and grabbed the receiver. "Hello!"

"GAAAGH." Someone or something gave a horrible croak on the other end of the line. Several horrible croaks. She held the receiver away from her ear.

"Who—or what is this?" she demanded.

"Scee-aagh!" The voice croaked some more, then got out something that sounded like "Shosh." No, it was "Josh."

"Dr. Williams, is that you? What's the matter?" Not that she was in any mood to talk to *him*. In the past few weeks since their "nudging" encounter in the conservatory, he'd been more impossible and ill tempered than ever. Today was Saturday. Wasn't she to have a respite from him?

But now his voice grew agitated. More hoarse croaks; it was like listening to an enraged frog.

"Slow down," Sara said, although she didn't know what good that would do. She couldn't understand a word he was saying. Finally he lowered his voice to a raspy whisper and became slightly more articulate.

"Bad cold. Voice gone," he managed.

"I should say so. I thought you looked under the weather this week. You ought to have some thistle tea and then go straight to bed."

"Dinner—Stuart Awards. Speech!"

"Oh, no, surely you're not thinking about that. You'll have to cancel." Sara found she was good at understanding Joshua's whispered shorthand. Tonight the Stuart Awards banquet would be held at the college. It was the Department of Biology's most prestigious event. Every autumn three awards were given out to students who had excelled in research during the previous year. Joshua was the faculty sponsor for two of the students who would be honored tonight and he was scheduled to give a speech.

"I know how much you wanted to be there," Sara went on. "But obviously you're in no condition. I'm sure everyone will understand—"

"No! Get over here. Groggy. Doctor. Medicine."

"Well, I'm glad you had enough sense to go to the doctor and get some medicine. But if it's making you that groggy, you're in no shape to go anywhere. Drink some orange juice along with your tea and settle down for the evening. Remember, it's thistle tea you want.

Or bugleweed tea, if you can't lay your hands on anything else.''

He started making hoarse squawks again. Sara winced, but finally he calmed down and went back to a scratchy whisper.

"Must attend. Can't disappoint students. You come. You drive."

"How the heck do you think you're going to sound up there at the podium? Be reasonable for once. Just listen to yourself—"

"Sara. You come. My house. Now!" He banged the receiver down in her ear.

She thumped down her own receiver and glared at the telephone. The man was infuriating. He'd been relentless these past weeks, piling extra work on her, making exorbitant demands. This last demand was the worst. He wasn't showing the least bit of common sense and she wouldn't give in to him. No way.

She crossed to the window, the floorboards of the drafty farmhouse creaking under her feet. She stared out at the wet gloom. It had been raining for days, soaking her cornfields. This was the last thing she needed right before harvest time. The ears of corn were safe and snug, wearing their shucks like raincoats. But whenever the sun decided to come out again, the ground would be too muddy for combining. She wouldn't be able to get the harvest in on schedule. And what about her bean fields? By this time of year the beans ought to have dried nicely, but with all the moisture they were in danger of turning to mold or of sprouting right in their pods.

She couldn't afford bad weather like this! It had kept her cooped in the house most of the day, uneasy, worried about her crops. She'd tried to stay productive—slogging across the yard to milk the goats, mucking out the barn, bringing the farm ledgers up to date, doing her homework. But it wasn't easy writing about corn production when her own cornfields faced potential disaster. Sometimes Sara felt as if her life were like a precariously built bird's nest: bits of straw and paper and string and twigs, all held together haphazardly and balanced at the top of a tree—but always in danger of toppling over with an unexpected gust of wind or torrent of rain.

Now it seemed that Joshua Williams was even more a threat to her well-being than bad weather. He'd crowded into her life with his tousled red hair, his silver gray eyes and his mismatched socks. He made her feel uncomfortable, dissatisfied; he made her realize how lonely she'd been ever since taking over the farm. She hadn't realized the loneliness before Joshua, but now it ached inside her. She felt a void in her life. But surely she didn't have room for Joshua—for his colorfulness and intensity and grouchiness. She didn't have the time to stand around remembering that one elusive moment among the palms and banyan trees of the conservatory, his lips brushing against hers....

Oh, damn, she wanted to go to him! A strange exhilaration swept through her, a conviction that she'd escape the rain and all her other worries if she went to his house tonight. It didn't make any sense, of course. He was the cause of most of her problems, not the solution. But even so, Sara turned and went to her bedroom with a sudden lightness of heart. She rummaged through her closet, wishing the pickings weren't so sparse. Her denim skirt, a few blouses and precisely two dresses . . . her clothes budget had been one of the first things to suffer when she'd taken over the farm.

Well, she'd have to be happy with her faithful standby, a shirtdress in red-and-black checkered flannel. She changed into it quickly, enjoying the soft, familiar touch of the flannel against her skin. The black leather belt was only slightly worn, and the folds of the skirt fell gracefully from the pleated waist to mid-calf. Perhaps the dress could benefit from a bit of ironing—but, no, she wasn't going to indulge *that* new compulsion. She slipped on her buckaroo boots, their black leather matching her belt perfectly. Only one thing left to do: comb her hair out until it crackled with electricity, shining in ripple after ripple from being braided all day.

Sara grabbed her slicker and dashed out to her big green truck. A few moments later she was rattling along the highway toward the town of Glenn Creek, lightning flashing around her, rain pounding her windshield until the arc of the wipers could barely sweep the water away. She sat hunched over the steering wheel, peering down the road. She'd given the truck its tune-up, but it still coughed and sputtered now and then. The bald tires were unsure on the slick pavement and Sara slowed carefully, traveling along like a finicky cat afraid to get its paws wet.

"Just hang on until December," Sara urged her truck. "In December everything will be better. I'll graduate and be accepted in the Farm Managers Program. I'll overhaul every single piece of equipment— finally open up the west fields, expand the goat herd— I'll be on my way!" It was a chant she repeated to herself, over and over. Hang on until December... that was all, hang on until December.

Her headlights cut a path through the rain, the last of dusk deepening toward night. Eventually she reached the outskirts of town; it took her much longer than usual because of the storm. Concrete grain elevators towered above her like giant smokestacks. Glenn Creek was a sprawling prairie town that serviced the surrounding farms as well as the agricultural college. Hidden far off in the distance were the peaks of the Rocky Mountains. The rivers flowing down from those mountains were what made the Colorado plains such fertile land for farming. But Sara didn't want to think about water of any type right now. The rain was pounding harder than ever, and she drove straight to Joshua's house.

She was ashamed to admit even to herself that she knew his address by heart, having looked it up in the telephone book several times. Good grief, that was the sort of thing teenage girls did! She was twenty-four years old, a woman with her own farm to run. But Joshua Williams brought out the most alarming tendencies in her.

He lived in a rambling house of burgundy brick, set well back from the street, with a wonderful big yard and plenty of trees. It was a private sort of place. Privacy... that seemed very important to Joshua. Sara held her slicker over her head and ran up to the front porch. She knocked a couple of times before Joshua came to the door. He didn't say a word—probably *couldn't* say a word. He ushered her inside, a lugubrious expression on his face. His eyes were bleary and

his nose a bright red, almost rivaling the color of his
hair.

"You look terrible," Sara pronounced. "You can't
possibly go anywhere tonight, especially in this
weather."

He gave an outraged squawk. But before Sara could
respond, an elderly dog rounded the sofa and hobbled toward her. It was a beautiful old collie with stiff
joints. Sara knelt down in front of it, holding out her
hand. The collie sniffed her fingers with a stately air,
then sat back abruptly on its haunches and wheezed
for breath.

"Oh, you're gorgeous," Sara murmured, stroking
the collie's ruff of sable fur. "And you've been around
for quite a long time, haven't you? A regular grandfather. Or maybe you're a grandmother."

"LAAGH," croaked Joshua.

Sara glanced up at him. "What was that?" she
asked politely, although she had absolutely no hope he
could make himself any clearer. Joshua went to a desk
in the corner, slapping papers around. Finally he re-
trieved a pad of scratch paper from all the clutter on
the desk, scribbled something on it and thrust it at
Sara.

"'Laddie,'" she read. "So your dog's name is
Laddie."

The collie thumped his tail as if to confirm this information.

"Pleased to meet you, Laddie." What a combination master and dog made—the two of them croaking
and squawking, wheezing and shuffling. Sara felt she
ought to pack both of them off to bed, a cup of this-

tle tea apiece. She straightened up, tossing her slicker onto the sofa.

"Darn it, Joshua, you're not leaving this house. You'll get pneumonia out there." It was the first time she'd called him anything but Dr. Williams; she was amazed at how easily his name slipped off her tongue. But it appeared nothing else would be easy tonight. Joshua's expression was growing more stubborn by the second. He began writing again on his scratch pad.

"'Can't disappoint my students. They're counting on me,'" Sara read. "Well, that's very noble and all, but I hardly think your students want you to catch your death. Besides, how are you going to give your speech—with flash cards? I'll call the school and explain everything."

"We're going!" Joshua bellowed hoarsely. He seemed surprised to have uttered something understandable. Surprised and very pleased with himself. He headed for the front door.

"Wait," Sara called. "All right, maybe I can't stop you from going tonight—unless I hit you over the head with a skillet or something. But at least do me a favor. Consider what you're wearing! Mismatched socks are one thing, but this time you've gone too far."

He glanced down at his brown corduroy jacket and his purple tie. It wasn't just any shade of purple. No, this reddish purple was almost fluorescent. It fairly glowed, as if Joshua had been attacked by a jar of radioactive grape jelly. But he didn't act like he noticed anything unusual.

"Color coordination isn't exactly your strong point, now, is it?" Sara hinted. "If you insist on going and

catching pneumonia, at least do it in something besides that horrible tie."

He opened his mouth, but this time not even the
slightest croak would come out. Joshua looked extremely disgruntled as he scrawled on his scratch pad,
using much greater force than necessary. It took Sara
a minute to decipher what he'd written.

"What's this word...'conk'? And this other
one...'blonk'? No, wait, I've got it. 'Color blind.'"
She stared at him. "You're color blind? Well, *that* ex-
plains your socks! Why didn't you say so before?
You're the most stubborn man alive, Joshua. It seems
you won't admit you're color blind unless you're absolutely forced into it. So you end up wearing things
like that—that grisly tie. Somebody ought to shoot it
and bury it before it causes any more damage."

He held up his watch and jabbed a finger toward it.

"Okay, I know we're late. But you'll have to let me
pick out another tie for you. That's all there is to it."

It was interesting to see how expressive a man's face
could become when he was deprived of his voice.
Joshua's eyebrows conveyed special perturbation,
shooting up and then downward again. But eventually he went along the hallway, Sara surmising that she
was to follow him. Laddie came last of all with his
shuffling gait, eager to be in on everything even
though he moved slower than a turtle.

Sara found herself led to Joshua's bedroom. The
intimacy here sent a delicious shiver down her spine:
this was the guilty pleasure of trespassing on forbidden territory. Joshua's bed was rumpled, the pillows
all tossed about as if he'd tried to subdue them but lost
the battle. And what bright sheets: vivid orange and

yellow. Sleeping in a bed like that, you'd feel you'd landed in a whole meadow of marigolds. A few casually framed prints hung on the walls. One of them was a lovely Monet, alive with subtle shadings of blue and green. It seemed odd that a man who was color blind would surround himself with so much color; perhaps any hues he *could* see were especially important to him. The world that Joshua Williams lived in was more a mystery to Sara than ever. How did he think—how did he see things? Maybe she'd never know, since he was such a private person. The realization made her feel more lonely than ever...and perversely determined to know him, no matter how he might try to shut her out.

He pulled a rack of ties from his closet and plunked it down on the bureau. More wild and exuberant colors! And patterns in paisleys, stripes, improbable yet delightful swirls. Sara chose a wool tie with gold and rust stripes, deciding it would go well with Joshua's corduroy jacket. When he took off the glowing purple tie, she grabbed it and stuffed it deep into the pocket of her dress. He scowled at her, but she refused to give it back. *Somebody* had to protect the man from himself.

Sara and Laddie watched as Joshua knotted the replacement tie. His fingers didn't move as deftly as usual; that medicine he'd taken must have really packed a wallop.

"At least you had the sense to call me instead of driving yourself," Sara told him. "And, you know, I almost like you like this—unable to talk, no matter what I say to you. I might even confiscate your notepad."

Joshua's eyebrows shot up again, but Laddie wheezed happily—as if to support Sara's plan. She leaned down and scratched the collie between his ears. Perhaps Joshua was a private man, but she could learn a lot about him just by observing the little things. For example, he was willing to keep on an ancient dog like this. It couldn't be easy. Sara remembered one of the farm dogs, a mutt who'd lived to be seventeen and who'd been at the vet's every other week for a whole variety of ailments. So it said something about Joshua Williams that he had an asthmatic old collie limping around after him. The man was surely more soft-hearted than he cared to let on.

But Joshua was already striding down the hall, showing some of his usual energy in spite of his cold. Sara hurried after him.

"Goodbye, Laddie," she called. She snatched up her slicker and once outside, she tried to hold it over both herself and Joshua so they wouldn't get wet. He shrugged it aside impatiently, allowing the rain to pelt him. Exasperated, Sara wanted to pelt him herself. Darn his pigheaded nature! Did he really want to get pneumonia?

In the truck she turned on the heater full blast and began chauffeuring Joshua to the college. "I have another theory about you," she said. "Want to hear it? Hold up two fingers for 'yes,' three for 'no.' Never mind, I'll tell you anyway." She ignored the three fingers he waggled in front of her face. "Okay, this is it. I think you find it very difficult to accept anything you perceive as a weakness in yourself. I mean, color blindness could happen to anybody. It's just a circumstance, like having blue eyes or being lefthanded or growing up to be six feet tall. But I really believe you think of it as a weakness. So you won't even acknowledge it. I can imagine what you're like in a store, buying shirts and things without telling the salespeople you need help. That's the way you handle it, isn't it?''

She could feel him glaring at her. This really was enjoyable, him not being able to talk back.

"Anyway," she went on cheerfully, "you're acting the same way with this cold. *Everyone* gets colds, but you're behaving as if you have to overcome it by sheer willpower. You won't do the sensible thing and give your body a chance to recuperate. You probably think of yourself as a sensible person, but you're really not. You're too stubborn to be sensible.''

He made a sound that was somewhere between a growl and a hoarse groan. Sara smiled to herself. This was the first time she'd actually had the upper hand with Joshua Williams. Too bad she couldn't take full advantage of the situation. She would've liked to keep right on driving, maybe all the way to Denver, treating Joshua to more of her theories about his personality. But here they were at the college. As soon as Sara parked, Joshua swung out of the truck and strode toward the biology building. Sara sprinted after him, flapping her slicker in vain. By the time Joshua reached the door of the building, he was soaked. He looked more miserable than ever, with his red nose and his hair plastered down over his forehead.

"For crying out loud," Sara muttered. She took the phosphorescent purple tie out of her pocket and tried to mop him up a little. He gave her one of his more eloquent frowns and headed into the common room.

He probably hoped Sara would wait outside for him like a good chauffeur. But she wasn't going to allow him *any* satisfaction tonight. She stayed right on his heels.

In spite of the weather, a good many people had turned out for the banquet. Tables had been set up throughout the common room and the guests were just beginning to sit down. Joshua wound his way among the tables, giving a brusque nod whenever anyone greeted him. No one seemed to find it odd when he didn't speak, didn't answer any of the questions flung his way; his gruff reputation was well-established by now. Sara shook her head in wonder. He probably preferred people to think he was rude than to let on he'd lost his voice. What on earth was he planning? Sooner or later everyone would have to know the truth.

He reached the head table, Sara beside him. When he pulled out a chair...she pulled out the chair next to him. He glared at her. She glared back. They both sat down at the same time.

Dr. Randolph, one of the other biology professors, reached over to shake Joshua's hand. "Hello there, Williams!" he boomed heartily. Dr. Randolph always boomed when he spoke—a disconcerting fact, because he was a short, skinny man who looked like an anemic tadpole. It was hard to understand how he could have such a big voice.

"Glad to see you brought a friend along, Williams," Dr. Randolph thundered. He squinted at Sara. "Don't I know you, young lady? Of course. Josh's research assistant. What do you know." His voice carried impressively far, as if he possessed his own in-

ternal megaphone. Several heads swiveled toward
Joshua and Sara with marked curiosity. Meanwhile,
the rest of Joshua's face turned as bright red as his
nose. He looked like he was going to explode.

"RAAAGH!" Joshua protested.

Dr. Randolph ignored this noise. "Wish my assistant was as dedicated as yours, Williams—and as
pretty." He gave Sara a fatherly wink.

Joshua picked up his fork and stabbed the air. But
whatever point he wanted to get across was lost on Dr.
Randolph. The Dean of Plant Sciences began giving
the opening speech and all attention centered on him.

Sara studied Joshua covertly. He was angry. Why in
tarnation was he overreacting like this to Dr. Randolph's silly but innocent remarks? Was she so loath-
some he couldn't tolerate even a hint that the two of
them might *like* each other? She gripped her own fork
until her knuckles turned white and she barely heard
a word uttered by the Dean of Plant Sciences.

Several freshman biology students began serving
dinner. Two of these students were pretty girls who
jostled each other for the opportunity to serve Joshua
his barbecued beef and cabbage rolls. The blasted man
was too good-looking—even his red nose attracted fe-
males like a light bulb drawing moths. One girl laid the
bread basket in front of him as if it were a sacred offering. Yet he seemed oblivious to this fawning. He
brought out his scratch pad, scribbled furiously on it
and stuck it in Sara's face. She read what he'd written: "Dammit, why are you pretending to be my
date?" The man could even swear on paper.

Sara snatched his pen and scribbled her own furious note. "I'm not pretending anything. You're the

one who called me up and ruined a perfectly good Saturday evening!''

"This is part of your job," he jotted back. "You're supposed to act like a professional."

Sara's answer was so forceful it almost tore through the notepad. "How can I act like a professional when you act like a cantankerous hippo?"

Dr. Randolph watched with interest as the two of them exchanged these impassioned notes. Now he'd really think something was going on between them— and it would be Joshua's fault, not hers!

She hardly touched her food and neither did Joshua. Dr. Randolph, however, ate steadily. When he was finished, he glanced speculatively at Joshua's plate as if ready to eat another whole dinner. Maybe Dr. Randolph could consume mountains of food and still remain skinny because all the calories went into stoking his big voice.

The two freshman girls fought over giving Joshua his blueberry pie for dessert. And then the Dean of Plant Sciences rose to speak again.

"Ladies and gentlemen, you all know how fortunate we are to have Dr. Joshua Williams on the faculty. His work on hybrid viability is a tremendous contribution to the agricultural sciences. At the same time, he is revitalizing our horticulture program and inspiring young biology students whose own research will someday make Glenn State proud. Ladies and gentlemen, I give you Dr. Joshua Williams!"

Applause sounded enthusiastically throughout the room. It seemed a contradiction that Joshua could be so popular on campus and also have a monumental reputation for being ill-humored. But that was exactly how it was.

Joshua obviously didn't like applause; he wore a very sour expression as he stood at the podium. He took out the notes for his speech and set them down in front of him. Sara watched nervously. What did he think would happen now? Did he truly believe his willpower was so strong he could command his own voice to obey? Too bad he couldn't borrow just a bit of Dr. Randolph's booming voice tonight.

Joshua attempted to clear his throat. He shuffled his notes. He opened his mouth and shut it again. He stared at the microphone in front of him with a belligerent expression, perhaps thinking he could cajole the thing into speaking for him. The crowd waited, respectfully silent. Not a sound came from Joshua, not even a raspy whisper. Sara leaned forward, almost holding her breath. How far did he think he could take this obstinate nonsense?

But then Joshua turned his head and looked straight at Sara. And something happened that she never would have expected. He sent her a wordless plea for help. She saw it clear as anything in his silvery gray eyes.

Yes . . . in front of an entire roomful of people, the almighty Joshua Williams was actually asking Sara for help.

CHAPTER FOUR

THAT ONE SILENT APPEAL from Joshua was enough. Without hesitation Sara pushed back her chair and stood. She marched right up to the podium, taking a place beside Joshua. At last the man was showing some sense. He'd asked Sara for help, and that was exactly what she intended to do—help him. For once matters between the two of them would be simple and straightforward.

Sara gave the audience what she hoped was a reassuring smile and leaned in front of the microphone. "Ladies and gentlemen, Dr. Williams regrets that he will not be able to deliver his speech personally to you tonight. He's suffering from laryngitis—" Sara stopped abruptly as Joshua poked her in the back. It was a protesting sort of poke, no doubt about it. She tried to ignore it and went on.

"Ladies and gentlemen, as I'm sure you'll all agree with me, anybody could get laryngitis. You won't hold it against Dr. Williams. And I'll be happy to read his speech for you." Sara reached over to take Joshua's notes, but he wouldn't hand them to her. Instead he frowned and began flipping through them as if they were a deck of cards and he was looking for the ace of spades. Just how obstinate was the man going to be?

He *had* asked for her help. Sara reached for the note cards again, only this time she got a firm hold and tugged them away from him. He scowled at her. She scowled back. Then she turned to the microphone once more.

"'Distinguished guests and honored students,'" she read. "'Tonight we are celebrating the spirit of curiosity that motivates every good scientist. When you think about it, a scientist is the nosiest person around. A snoop, a meddlesome prier, a busybody of the most unashamed sort.'" A murmur of laughter went through the audience, and Sara smiled, too. She continued.

"'We therefore must encourage our students to pry and learn, then to pry some more with that unquenchable spirit of curiosity. We must encourage any—'" Goodness, what was the next word? Sara peered down at Joshua's handwriting. He'd gone on quite legibly for a few lines and then suddenly his words had exploded on the paper as if he'd gotten overly excited about his train of thought. Now she held the note cards up closer to her nose. "'We must encourage any—'"

Joshua prodded her, obviously trying to maneuver her away from the podium. The man had no patience; he wouldn't give her a chance to decipher his wild handwriting. But she held her ground. Joshua prodded her again and she stared at him in exasperation.

"Hang it, Joshua, let me read the blasted speech!" Too late did she realize how the microphone had carried her voice, her indignant words echoing in the room. Joshua only made matters worse. He confiscated his note cards, then angled his way in front of the microphone.

"Ladies and gentlemen," he managed to rasp out, with a great deal of effort. He was actually attempting it. He was too bullheaded to accept Sara's help. But he was going to get her help, whether he liked it or not. Craning her neck, she managed to speak into the microphone.

"Ladies and gentlemen, let's indeed celebrate the spirit of curiosity tonight. The Dean of Plant Sciences will now present awards to three students who have been truly inquisitive. Please give those students a hearty round of applause!"

The audience's response definitely had a relieved sound to it, and Joshua had no choice but to vacate the podium with Sara. As they both sat down again, she could feel his blood pressure rising; his expression had become ominous.

The dean finished presenting the awards, more applause followed—and then all attention at the head table seemed to focus on Joshua. Everyone had an opinion.

"So, Williams, can't talk? At a real loss for words, are you? Heh, heh! Uh, sorry. Just a little joke there. Couldn't help myself...."

"You look awful, Dr. Williams. Really sick. And I mean really sick. You never should've come out on a night like this. Dear me. What on earth were you thinking?"

"I'm sure you don't eat enough carrots, that's your problem. I eat at least one carrot every day and I *never* get sick. When was the last time you had a carrot, Dr. Williams?''

Joshua's expression turned even grimmer. It was obvious he didn't appreciate comments about his appearance or inquiries into his eating habits. He brought out his scratch pad again and jotted a vitriolic note to Sara: ''Why the devil did you have to blab about my voice? Look what you did.''

Sara jotted back, ''Did you think no one would find out? Everybody's sympathetic, so just be grateful.''

His answer was emphatic, scrawled boldly across the notepad. ''I HATE SYMPATHY.''

At last the banquet was officially over. Sara hurried Joshua out of the building and across the rainy parking lot to her truck. She was very glad to be leaving the banquet behind—very glad, indeed. It hadn't exactly been a resounding success in her career as Joshua Williams's assistant. The man was impossible!

Sara cranked the engine, but her tired old truck refused to start. She pumped the gas.

''Flaagh,'' said Joshua grumpily from the passenger side. Sara found she was getting better and better at interpreting him.

''Don't worry, I won't flood it,'' she replied. ''I know how to coax this baby. She just needs a little time.'' Sara cursed under her breath as the truck still refused to start. ''You drove me nuts in there,'' she said, taking out her frustrations on Joshua. ''I would've handled everything fine, if you had simply let me do my job. I wish I could figure you out for once. These last few weeks you've had me working on

any nitpicking, insignificant little job you could dream
up to aggravate me. But tonight, when it was really
important for me to help you—well, you balked.
That's what you did. You balked."

"Haagh!"

"Believe me, I'd like nothing better than to get you
to your house as soon as possible and be rid of you."
Sara pumped the gas again and her old truck sputtered to life. "But you should appreciate the concern
of all those people. This is a very friendly and caring
school. It's something special."

"AAAGH!"

Sara didn't think that even deserved an answer. She
rattled out of the parking lot, her windshield wipers
slapping away. The rain was coming down harder than
ever. It took all her concentration to keep her bald tires
steady on the wet pavement. After the strain of the
evening, her nerves were frazzled. The weather didn't
help one bit. By the time she pulled the truck into
Joshua's driveway, her whole body was tense from
clutching the steering wheel. The only thing she
wanted now was to get home, away from Joshua Williams. But he *was* sick. He coughed in a way that made
Sara wince. And when she turned off her engine, he
simply sat in the truck as if he didn't have the energy
to get out and walk to his front door. No wonder; he'd
already used up all his energy just being stubborn tonight.

Sara slid down from her own side of the truck and
went around to Joshua. He stirred in a grouchy manner, barely managing to crawl out. Sara held her
slicker over both of them, hauling him up the walk and

into his house. Once inside he yawned wearily, his eyelids drifting downward. Sara was afraid he'd fall asleep on his feet. Before she could lose her momentum, she propelled him along the hallway to his bedroom. Laddie, the elderly collie, shuffled after them as if to give moral support.

Joshua sat down heavily on his bed, staring at the floor. By this stage he seemed oblivious to Sara. She took his legs and swung them up onto the bed. He collapsed backward without even one protest. Slipping off his loafers Sara noted that tonight, at least, his socks matched. By the time she pulled the covers over him, he was snoring. She stood looking down at him for a moment. Even in sleep the man looked stubborn, with his unruly red hair, obstinate nose and forceful eyebrows. The oddest sensation tingled through Sara: a tantalizing warmth she couldn't explain. Joshua Williams had given her a thoroughly wretched evening—yet here she was, dawdling beside his bed.

His head moved on the pillow and he frowned as if displeased with Sara even in his dreams. Didn't the man ever lighten up? She hadn't wanted to spend this crazy evening with him. It hadn't been her choice at all. His frown deepened and Sara frowned back at him. Then she clicked off the light and marched out to the living room.

The rain hadn't let up one bit. Water streamed against the windows as if someone had turned on a giant hose outside. Sara wanted to leave Joshua's house right this minute, but unfortunately she had to use some common sense. Her old truck wouldn't be safe on the road until the storm subsided a little. Giving a vigorous sigh, she plopped down in an armchair. Laddie had padded after Sara and she leaned over and gave the collie a good scratch behind the ears. She was happy to have Laddie's company. It helped to keep her mind off the unsettling fact that Joshua was sleeping down the hall.

Sara relaxed and glanced around the living room. The atmosphere was surprisingly homey, with a brick fireplace, an ancient sofa upholstered in a vivid pattern of green and orange leaves, several glass-fronted bookshelves crowding each other for space. The outside of Joshua's house might be sober and restrained, but inside it was filled with all sorts of colorful details—rather like Joshua himself.

He was a perplexing man, trying to present himself as nothing but a coolheaded scientist. Hah! He wasn't coolheaded in the least, especially when dealing with Sara. Around her he surpassed his own reputation for being cantankerous and unreasonable. Every single day he made it clear that he still wanted to be rid of her. But why? That was what she needed to know. Why did he behave as if he couldn't tolerate her? Over and over she'd proven herself to be a good worker. What more did he want? All right, so she'd slipped up that one time; she'd kissed him that day in the conservatory. It hadn't been a professional thing to do. She'd be the first one to admit that. But she was darn sorry it had happened. She hadn't slipped up since. And she deserved a little better treatment from the almighty Dr. Joshua Williams.

Sara tapped her boots against the wooden floor. Laddie raised his head and gave her an inquiring look. She reached down to pet him.

"Sorry, boy," she murmured. "Got myself all worked up over your master. I don't think it'll do me any good, though." Sara stared out the window, where the rain poured down more violently than ever. It appeared she still had a wait ahead of her. Shivering, she took an afghan from the sofa. Then she propped her feet on an ottoman and spread the afghan over her legs. It was made of brightly colored squares, the sort of thing an aunt or grandmother might crochet. Sara wondered if, indeed, some elderly aunt had crocheted this afghan as a gift for Joshua.

Sara closed her eyes. Maybe if she knew more about Joshua, she'd be able to figure out why he'd taken such an intense and personal dislike to her. Sara wasn't used to being disliked. She had to figure it out...later. Right now she was beginning to feel warm and cozy, the rain drumming down on the roof but unable to reach her. She was so tired from her hectic schedule. This was an unplanned respite—but still, it was a respite. She'd keep her eyes closed only a few moments longer....

SARA SHIFTED IN HER CHAIR. She could feel lovely, warm sunlight against her eyelids. No sound of rain came from outside; perhaps the storm was over at last. Her muscles were cramped from sleeping in this armchair, but she was reluctant to get up. She kept her eyes closed. Ironically, this was the best patch of sleep she'd had in months, sitting here all hunched over in Joshua

Williams's living room. She smiled at the humor of it, stretching her arms.

Wait a minute! That was the sun? Had she slept here all *night?* Sara's eyes flew open in horror. She saw two faces gazing at her. One was a long, narrow collie face that looked happy to see her. The other was all too human and disapproving...the disgruntled face of Dr. Joshua Williams.

"What the devil are you still doing here?" he said in a hoarse voice.

Sara struggled into a more upright position, pushing aside the afghan. "I don't mean to be here—I only thought I'd doze for a second—goodness, you can talk. You sound dreadful, but you can talk. Isn't that fantastic?"

"Yeah, right. It's a miracle. I want you out of my house, Ms. Bennett. Now."

She stood up, smoothing her wrinkled dress and pushing a tangle of hair away from her face. She wished for the neat braid she usually wore. "At least let me explain why I'm still here. You see, it was raining so hard I—"

"No explanations necessary. Just leave." Joshua rubbed his hands through his own hair, as if trying to work the cobwebs out of his brain—and work Sara out of his sight. No matter what, he did look better than he had last evening. This morning his eyes were clear, his skin no longer flushed with fever.

"I *am* leaving," Sara said, grabbing up her rain slicker. "My goats are waiting to be milked, after all. But here's the thing. I couldn't possibly have gone home last night while it was still pouring. My truck never would've made it. So I sat down and thought I'd rest for just a minute—''

"Great. You're all rested up...and the rain's stopped. Now, goodbye.'' Joshua coughed and loosened the tie he was still wearing—the tie in gold-and-rust stripes that Sara had chosen for him. Gold and rust brown, those were good colors for Joshua. They highlighted the russet of his hair and hinted at the earthiness that seemed an essential part of his nature. The man radiated vibrancy, even in the aftermath of a cold. Sara lingered beside him, clutching her rain slicker.

"Are you ever going to leave my house, Sara?''

"Absolutely. Can't wait to get out of here.'' She turned to go, just as the doorbell rang. Joshua rasped out an oath.

"Who the hell is that?'' he demanded. "Isn't anybody going to leave me in peace?''

"I guess you're just too popular,'' Sara said dryly. "But I'll answer and see who it is. I'll send them away, since you're sick.'' She started toward the front door, disconcerted when Joshua took hold of her arm and wheeled her around in the opposite direction. He ferried her down the hall toward the back of his house with an obvious sense of purpose.

"What are you doing?''

"Use your head, Ms. Bennett. Think it through. You answer my door early Sunday morning, and what'll happen next? A bunch of damn rumors, that's what. A bunch of rumors about me and my *too* pretty assistant. Well, I've had it with that kind of trouble. No more. It's not going to happen again!''

"I don't know what you're talking about," Sara protested. "All right, I agree this...um, circumstance might seem a little awkward to someone else. Me staying at your house overnight and everything. But it has such a logical explanation. And I'd be glad to explain—"

"You've been trying to explain things since the minute I found you camped out in my living room. And you haven't done a very good job." Joshua ushered her unceremoniously into a room near the end of the hall. "There. Stay here and be quiet. I'll clean up this mess you've started." Joshua clapped the door of the room shut on her, leaving her with his humiliating instruction to "be quiet."

What possessed the man? He was only making things worse by hiding her in here. It had never been her intention to fall asleep in his house! It had simply happened. The last thing *she* needed was to start rumors. But the solution was to be straightforward about the whole thing. Whoever was outside ringing the bell would understand. Sara would explain about the storm and about the bald tires on her truck and about how tired she'd been these last few weeks. It was all perfectly innocent and anyone sensible would be able to see that.

Sara glared at the door, thinking about what Joshua had said—about how he'd had enough of rumors. "That kind of trouble," he'd called it. And he'd declared that it wasn't going to happen to him again. Just now Joshua had let slip a very important detail. At some point in the past, he'd had to deal with rumors about one of his assistants. Sara could only speculate what those rumors had been. She needed to get the full story out of Joshua. The story might help her understand a lot of things about him ... yes, it might help her understand a lot.

Sara pressed her ear to the door, but as she couldn't hear a word of what was happening on the other side of the thick oak panel, she glanced around to see where Joshua had left her. The huge desk proclaimed this as Joshua's study. The man certainly had a penchant for big, unwieldy desks. And this room was almost as cluttered as his office at the college—bookshelves everywhere, an elaborate computer in the middle of all the papers on the desk, a sturdy exercise bike taking up one corner. Sara wandered restlessly in front of the crowded bookshelves, scanning titles. More volumes on American history, a dog-eared text on woodworking, the complete plays of Shakespeare ... and a scrapbook with a faded leather cover. Joshua Williams actually *did* keep a scrapbook. Sara couldn't resist turning the pages. They were filled with black-and-white photographs: pictures of a rather frazzled-looking couple with two little girls and a young boy. Sara recognized the boy immediately as Joshua. The rumpled hair and disgruntled expression were the same. Even at the age of eight or nine he'd gazed sternly into the camera with a "don't-push-me" warning in his eyes.

Here were pictures of the two little girls tap-dancing in absurdly ruffled costumes and singing a duet beside a piano. These had to be Joshua's sisters, the ones who had grown up to be "flappers" in a nightclub act. And here were more pictures of the young Joshua. In one photograph he was holding a violin awkwardly under his chin; in another he was executing a tap dance himself, all dressed up in an old-fashioned double-breasted suit, complete with top hat and cane. Once again, Joshua was scowling belligerently. It was very clear that as a kid, he'd not only hated being in front of the camera—he'd hated tap-dancing.

Sara turned the next page, curious to see what else she'd find. But then the door of the room swung open. Joshua stood in the doorway, wearing the same ominous scowl he'd perfected as a child. He was holding a jar of some dark, murky liquid, looking as if he was about to toss it out the window.

"Ms. Bennett, you've really made my day," he grumbled hoarsely. "Thanks to you, it seems every single person from the college knows I'm sick. I've just been held hostage in my own living room by one of the biology secretaries. She tried to pour this crud down my throat." He jiggled the jar of murky liquid. "Said it was some kind of cockeyed remedy. Said it would cure me right away. From the look of the stuff, more likely it'd kill me...what the hell do you have there?"

"It's your scrapbook."

"Put that damned thing down. You're not supposed to look at that." He waved his arm so emphatically that he almost sent his remedy sloshing out of its jar.

Sara remained stubbornly holding on to the scrapbook. "Listen, you're the one who hustled me in here, remember? And so it was only natural that I...well, I looked around a little. It's nothing for you to get all bent out of shape about. I think it's great that you tap-danced when you were a kid. I'm starting to find out all these things about you and it makes you seem so much more ... human.''

Joshua strode over to Sara, took the scrapbook from her and crammed it back into place on the shelf. He gave her such a sour look, you'd think he'd actually had to swallow that frightful remedy, after all.

''Ms. Bennett, you're the one who's going to be dancing. You're going to dance your way right out of my house!''

CHAPTER FIVE

"I'VE FOUND YOU OUT, Dr. Williams. You might as
well accept it. Do you still remember how to tap-
dance? That's what I'd like to know." Sara couldn't
resist teasing Joshua a little, but apparently he didn't
appreciate her sense of humor. He drew his expressive eyebrows together.

"Ms. Bennett, it's none of your concern whether I
can dance the watusi or the confounded cha-cha-cha.
Your only job right now is to get out of my house." He
took her arm and began escorting her firmly from the
room. Once he had her out in the hallway, he slammed
the door, and began moving her along at a good clip.
She gazed behind her resentfully, convinced so many
more of his secrets lurked inside that room.

"All right, tell me at least one thing," she said. "I
know something bad happened with you and some
other assistant of yours. You've already said as much.
And I think you ought to tell me the rest. Because
whatever happened with this other assistant is affecting your relationship with *me*. If we discuss it, maybe
we can clear up some of the difficulties between us."
Sara thought she was being more than reasonable, but
Joshua brought her up short and frowned.

"Ms. Bennett, the last thing in the world I'm going to do is explain what happened with...never mind. Don't ask again. It's none of your business."

Was that bitterness Sara glimpsed behind the anger in Joshua's eyes? She couldn't tell for sure. "I believe it *is* my business. Because it's affecting how you treat me. Just now, for instance—the way you hid me in that room because you're so afraid someone is going to assume the wrong thing about us. If you'd thought about it some more, you would've realized what a mistake it was. My truck is parked outside, Joshua. That secretary might figure out I was here no matter what. And then she'd be suspicious. She'd wonder why you were hiding me. Don't you see? Your judgment is being distorted by whatever happened to you in the past." Sara stopped, a little breathless with her own intensity. As she crammed her hands into the pockets of her dress, her fingers brushed the wadded-up purple tie she'd confiscated from Joshua last night. She was about to give it back to him, but already he was propelling her out the front door.

"Stop trying to analyze me, Ms. Bennett. You're lousy at it. Goodbye!"

And now she was out on the front stoop, watching as Joshua Williams banged yet another door in her face. Sara tightened her fingers around that miserable tie in her pocket and shivered in the cool early morning air. Realizing she'd left her rain slicker inside his house, she leaned on the doorbell for a long moment. Joshua didn't answer. Well, that was hardly surprising, given the man's stubborn disposition.

Sara went down the walk, then swiveled around and glared for another moment at Joshua's brick house.

Awnings hung low over the windows like protective eyelids. Joshua was determined to be so darn secretive. But some secrets had a habit of festering, and contaminating everything around them; too bad he didn't realize that.

She cut across the wet grass and swung into her truck. The engine coughed, sounding as sick and cranky as Joshua. She pumped the gas pedal and at last the engine steadied out. Sara turned the heater up to high. Perhaps Joshua had her rain slicker, but she had his purple tie. It was probably as fair a trade as she would ever get from him.

"Hopeless man," she muttered, backing out of his driveway. "I'm going home to my goats. At least they know how to treat a person!" With that Sara bumped onto the road and began the trip out of town—back to her farm, where she belonged.

SARA KNELT IN THE greenhouse and ran one finger gently along the skinny stem of her "giraffe" plant. "Okay, little guy," she murmured. "You're doing fine. Keep up the good work."

Sara could sense Joshua's presence behind her even before he spoke. "Gabbing to the plants again, Ms. Bennett? I'm not sure I want you messing with their minds. It might skew my research data." He crouched down and took the plant from her, gazing at it with a perplexed expression.

"Something's definitely wrong," he muttered. "This is the seedling you potted that first day. And it's grown taller than the others...the ones I potted. Doesn't make any sense."

"Yes, it does. Because I give my giraffe extra encouragement. It knows how much I care—"

"Spare me, Ms. Bennett. I'll find a logical explanation for the discrepancy—nitrogen or magnesium variations, soil temperature, whatever. I don't need to hear any of your crackbrained theories about how you communicate with your little green friends."

"Say, I like that. Plants—my green friends. I hadn't quite thought of it like that before, but you've described exactly how I feel."

Joshua gave her a look that would have withered a wax flower. "I'll finish up here," he said brusquely, his voice still somewhat hoarse from his cold. "You can get started on netting those moss poles."

Sara nodded, yet she lingered beside Joshua. She couldn't understand why she'd even want to be near him at all. He'd been more irascible than ever since the fiasco of the awards banquet the weekend before. And he'd been piling more and more busy work on her. Today she'd spent the entire afternoon at the library, researching obscure journal articles on the subject of ghost-fly control in greenhouses—even though Joshua himself was probably the foremost authority on ghost flies and greenflies and any other blasted fly that chose to feed off helpless plants.

Now Sara's eyes were aching from all those hours of squinting at faded typescript. She patted her fingers in the soil of another giraffe plant. As always, the feel of moist dirt helped to soothe her.

"It really is true," she told Joshua. "The seedling I potted *is* growing taller than the rest. Instead of giving me useless work to do, you ought to turn over this entire research project to me. I'd make it a big success."

Joshua didn't answer. He stuck a narrow tube of blue plastic deep into the soil of one of the giraffe plants. Then he poured a few drops of milky liquid into the tube from a vial.

"You're experimenting on that poor plant like it's a—a laboratory rat or something. It's not fair for you to force your bizarre formulas on innocent, unsuspecting greenery."

Joshua gave her another sour glance. "I'll try to be gentle. Now, could you get to work?"

"I wish you'd take me seriously for once. It's a proven scientific fact that plants can experience pain and furthermore—"

"Ms. Bennett, you're the one who's giving *me* a pain. Go take care of the moss poles."

"I don't think you'd be so irritable all the time if you talked about what was bothering you. You've got to bring it out in the open—this complex you have about research assistants."

"So now I have a 'complex.' Lord, let me guess. You're taking psychology this semester."

"No, actually, I'm not," Sara said. "But I took it when I was a freshman. And believe me, Dr. Williams, you show a classic case of maladjusted interpersonal behavior."

"Moss poles, Ms. Bennett!"

Sara sat back on the heels of her boots. Suddenly she couldn't force herself to do one more petty little job at the command of Dr. Joshua Williams. She was tired and on edge. She hadn't had a decent night's sleep since her snooze in Joshua's armchair, she was only halfway finished with her seminar paper on crop rotation, the goats were overdue to have their hooves trimmed and she couldn't get her harvest in because the ground was still too wet for combining. If she didn't get her crops in soon, she'd be ruined. With all this on her mind, she simply couldn't tolerate the thought of rolling a bunch of sawed-off broom handles in wire netting for Joshua. He already had plenty of moss poles lined up there against the wall, ready for philodendrons or any other climbing plants that needed a good support.

Sara herself needed a good support. She leaned back against a table leg, happy to find herself surrounded by gloxinia and pink impatiens and African violets. She was surprised when Joshua didn't snarl at her for sitting around. His policy at the moment seemed to be one of ignoring her. He went on kneeling there, working away with his tubes of plastic and his strange vials of liquid. Sara decided this was officially her coffee break, the first she'd taken since signing on with Joshua. She deserved this break, darn it all. So she settled back more comfortably, stretching out her legs in their faded jeans, and she watched Joshua. He moved deftly, competent in everything he did. His hands were big and powerful, but Sara had to admit he was careful with each seedling. He handled the plants in a matter-of-fact yet respectful fashion.

"You know," she said, "I think you have a lot more regard for a plant's feelings than you're willing to let on."

He turned to look at her, but he didn't say anything. He merely gazed at her, brow furrowed. He went on gazing, and Sara's heart began to thump uncomfortably. She ran her palms over her jeans, unable to look away. Joshua's eyes actually seemed to soften a little, more smoky gray now than silver gray. His gaze traveled to her mouth. And that was when she knew. She knew, without one single doubt, that Joshua was thinking about kissing her. He was contemplating a kiss....

Sara contemplated it, too. Heat suffused her face. The air of the greenhouse was heavy and humid—tropical air. Sara knew Joshua's lips would be warm against hers. Oh, yes, his kiss would be tropical. She leaned toward him a little. And it seemed he was bending toward her, doing his part to close the distance between them. But then he muttered an oath under his breath. He stood up so abruptly that Sara was left staring at his legs in their brown corduroy trousers.

"All right," he said. "That's it. Ms. Bennett, in my office. Now. We're going to straighten out this situation once and for all."

She scrambled to her feet and hurried after him as he strode from the greenhouse. Outside in the courtyard the cold autumn wind swirled around her, sweeping away any remnants of tropical dreams. Dry leaves scurried along the walk in front of Joshua, as if to escape the ominous tread of his feet. Sara jogged to catch up with him, scattering more leaves.

"You know, I've been wanting to clear things up all along," she said. "That's why I keep asking you about this other research assistant of yours. I hope you've finally decided to tell me what happened."

"I have plenty to tell you, Ms. Bennett." He yanked open the door of the biology building, gesturing her inside. His expression was grim, but that was nothing unusual. Sara wouldn't let it faze her. She gave him a determined smile and led the way into his office. She sat down in front of his big oak desk. He swung around to the other side, his swivel chair creaking as he thumped himself into it.

"I'm ready to hear your story," Sara informed him. "Start at the very beginning."

"There won't be any stories today. I brought you in here to show you this." He slapped a form across the desk and Sara picked it up. As she scanned it, she felt an icy coldness that had nothing to do with the autumn weather.

"This is Personnel Action Notice B-29. You're trying to terminate me! I can't believe it...."

"Don't get melodramatic. Officially, that's a transfer request. I'm requesting you be assigned to another assistantship. Since I'm a straightforward person, I'm telling you about it right off."

Slowly she lowered the form, crumpling a corner of it. "You have to give a reason when you terminate someone. Because that's what it is, Dr. Williams. I don't care what else you want to call it—you're trying to fire me. What reason are you going to give the dean and the employee committee and the liaison board and the advisory council?"

"The bureaucracy in this place," Joshua grumbled. "They probably have a committee to decide when to open and close the windows. But don't worry. I'm fair. I'll put down something vague on that form, something that won't incriminate you. I'll say that you and I are incompatible."

Sara almost laughed. Incompatible—it was the sort of word a married couple might use when splitting up. What a perverse joke to apply that same word to the exasperating, downright infuriating relationship between Joshua and herself. She slapped the form back on the desk.

"Am I supposed to be grateful that you only plan to *vaguely* incriminate me, Joshua? Because that's what you're doing. You're implying that I'm guilty of something. So just tell me what it is. Let's have this out! What exactly is your complaint about me?"

His eyes held a dangerous glint. "Okay, Sara, you want it out—we'll have it out. First, there was the incident in the conservatory. What you called a 'lip nudging.'"

"I thought we'd put that behind us," she said defensively. "It truly was an accident."

"I was ready to forget about it. But then you decided to spend the night at my house."

"I didn't decide—"

"Right. It was another accident. You're too damn accident-prone, Ms. Bennett. That's your problem."

Sara scooted to the edge of her seat, trying to get into a position where Joshua's big desk wouldn't seem such an obstacle. She was convinced that Joshua had this enormous, unwieldy desk in his office so that he could intimidate people. He sat behind it like a judge ready to mete out punishment for crimes. Well, Sara was no criminal, and she wouldn't be intimidated.

"I never would've fallen asleep at your house if you hadn't insisted on going to that banquet. It was a foolhardy thing to do when you were so sick. If you'd been at all reasonable that night I could have been home, minding my own business. Don't blame me because you're a mule-headed, dictatorial—''

"You're getting off the subject. That night you spent at my house has had serious repercussions. In case you haven't figured it out yet, there's been talk in the biology department about you and me. Disturbing talk."

Sara bit her lip. These past few days she'd been much too aware of the speculative glances thrown her way and the murmured conversations that stopped abruptly whenever she and Joshua entered a room together.

"The only thing to do about rumors is to ignore them," she said. "They'll die down soon enough."

"Unfortunately, rumors like that don't die down. They have a way of growing and causing all sorts of damage." He grimaced and again Sara wondered if she saw bitterness shadowing his face. It was difficult to tell with him; he kept all emotions except for grouchiness under tight control.

"You and I both know we haven't done anything wrong," she insisted. "That's the important thing. We can't give in to other people's imaginations. And if you fill out this—this form, that's exactly what you'll be doing. Giving in!" Sara pointed one finger at the offending document, too incensed by the thing to actually touch it.

Joshua tapped a pen against his desk, looking perturbed. "Believe it or not, I don't want to give these rumors any credence. That's why I've delayed filing a personnel-operation report on you...."

"Personnel-action notice," she corrected him dryly. "Form B-29. Aptly named, don't you think? Seeing that it involves dropping a bomb on your research assistant.''

''You're being melodramatic again. The truth is, since Monday I've debated about whether or not to file this report—this notice or whatever they want to call it. But what happened today made up my mind. Today you went too far, Ms. Bennett.''

She tensed. ''What are you talking about?''

''You know damn well. A few minutes ago in the greenhouse. You were getting all set for another 'nudging.' ''

Sara flushed. ''This is one case where you absolutely *can't* fob off the blame on me. You started it, Joshua. You looked at me and thought about kissing me and quite naturally the thought skipped along over.''

''Ms. Bennett, we're not talking about a game of mental leapfrog here.''

''No. What we're talking about is you refusing to take responsibility for your own kissing impulses.''

He groaned and ran both hands through his rumpled hair. ''Why can't the two of us have a rational dialogue? Tell me that.''

''What you really want is an easy way to fire your perfectly competent research assistant.'' Sara could no longer remain seated; the sprawling oak desk was too oppressive. She stood, wanting to shove the desk right out of the office. But that would have been impossible—it was too big to fit through the door.

''How did you get this monstrosity in here?'' she demanded.

''What the devil are you talking about now?''

"Your desk. It's hulking in here like a giant ship squeezed into a bottle. You probably insisted you had to have *this* particular desk, whether or not it would fit. You probably had people blasting out walls just so they could push it into your office."

"Ms. Bennett, are you trying to make a point?"

"Darn right I am. The point is that you refuse to admit any weaknesses. You refuse to admit this stupid desk is too big. And you refuse to admit that you wanted to kiss me in the greenhouse!" Sara pulled on her long braid, as if to anchor herself. She was getting too worked up and she knew it. So much was at stake with this job of hers; she had to remain cool. But Joshua Williams brought out the worst in her. He aggravated her no end. Right now, for instance, he was gazing at her with narrowed eyes, his mouth narrowed, too, in an unyielding line. Someone ought to snap a photograph of the man, hang it on the wall and call it "Portrait of Stubbornness." He wasn't going to admit the truth, that much was obvious.

"Dr. Williams, you pride yourself so much on having moral integrity. It's very important to you, I can tell that. But there are all sorts of integrity. What about having enough honesty to say what was really going through your mind, there in the greenhouse?" She waited for his answer, leaning on the desk as if she could subdue it into a more manageable size. At last Joshua spoke.

"All right, dammit," he said in a very gruff voice. "I confess. I wanted to kiss you. I wanted to kiss you like anything. Are you satisfied, Ms. Bennett?"

She was startled. She hadn't actually expected him to say those words. Spoken out loud, they were almost too tangible. It seemed that any second the thought of Joshua's kiss might turn into a real caress— in spite of the disgruntled expression on his face. Sara straightened up quickly.

"Well...at least we're finally getting some things into the open."

"What the hell good will that do us? I never trust people who want to get things out in the open. It's a bad sign, right off." Joshua pulled out one of his desk drawers and stared dourly into it, as if looking for a solution to the problem of Sara. Apparently he didn't find anything to inspire him and he shut it again with a good bang.

Sara sank back down in her chair. "From now on I hope we can discuss this matter logically. It appears that you're attracted to me and I'm attracted to you and...so forth. It's inconvenient and certainly not something either one of us wants, but we can resolve it. I know we can! Without resorting to Form B-29."

"There isn't any other way."

"People are attracted to each other all the time," Sara argued. "People who *shouldn't* be attracted to each other. But they deal with it. They get over it and they go on."

"I'm dealing with it, Ms. Bennett, by filling out Form B-29 in quadruplicate or quintuplicate or whatever the hell they want from me. Here goes." Joshua took the wretched form and began scrawling across it in his bold handwriting.

Sara didn't know what to do—how to stop him. She took a deep breath, trying to calm herself. But everything was on the line with this job...everything! She'd already allocated her paychecks clear through Christmas for one necessity or another. Storage space for this year's corn at the grain company, payment on the overdue vet bill, repairs to the barn roof, a new milk stand for the goats... all of that and more depended on the generous salary she made as Joshua's research assistant. And that generous salary could be the difference between success or failure for the farm.

Thinking hard, Sara smoothed out a thread that was unraveling from her vest. It was a vest her mother had knitted for her father years ago in soft blue wool. Sara's mother hadn't been very adept at knitting; the vest had sagged awkwardly from the first day and it still sagged. But it was one of Sara's favorite items of clothing, something she'd inherited from her parents just as she'd inherited the farm. In fact, Sara had been entrusted with the farm by her parents and her grandparents and her great-grandparents before that. She couldn't allow Joshua Williams to jeopardize the trust she'd been given.

"It all comes down to one thing," she told him. "It boils down to whatever happened to you before with that other research assistant. If only you'd talk about it. You could tell me what happened and then maybe you'd be able to see that the situation between us is entirely different."

He glanced up and for a moment stopped writing on that horrible form. "This situation *is* different," he said, his voice harsh. "Very different. You see, Sara, I wasn't attracted to that other research assistant. Not in the least. And I still ran into trouble. With you—it's a whole new set of problems. Problems I can't afford to have. So let's get the bureaucracy rolling on your transfer." He began writing once more, his pen so forceful it almost tore through the paper.

Sara found another thread unraveling on her vest. She was appalled at the fierce pleasure that rushed through her, just knowing that Joshua was attracted to her. How could she feel this way when her livelihood was on the line? No, more than her livelihood— her family legacy. She couldn't go all moonstruck about that almost-kiss in the greenhouse. Somehow she had to keep this job!

Slowly she began to realize exactly what she needed to do.

CHAPTER SIX

DAISY WAS RESTLESS TODAY. The little goat had already finished the oats in the feedbox and she didn't want to be milked anymore. She tried to wiggle her head out of the stanchion in the milking shed.

"Just a few more minutes," Sara murmured to the doe in a soothing voice as she squeezed Daisy's milk into the pail with deft fingers. Turning slightly, Sara glanced out the open door. And what she saw almost made her knock over her pail.

Dr. Joshua Williams was striding angrily across the field toward her. At least, he was attempting to stride angrily. It seemed he couldn't move very fast because Laddie, his elderly collie, was hobbling along behind him. He would take a few belligerent strides, pause for Laddie to catch up—and then he'd take a few more strides. Even from here Sara could see the scowl on his face.

She pushed back the brim of her seed cap and rose, then she released Daisy from the stanchion. The doe clattered down the ramp of the milking stand, heading out of the shed and straight for Joshua. Another goat converged on him, too, a kid with a glossy black coat and big, floppy white ears. By the time Sara herself came out, Joshua had a goat nuzzling him on either side. Laddie didn't seem too sure about the goats, hanging back behind his master. Joshua didn't seem sure about the goats, either. He looked more grouchy than ever.

"Can't you control these animals?" he demanded. Daisy was nibbling his shirtsleeve and Amaryllis, the kid, had poked her nose into the pocket of Joshua's corduroy trousers.

"Goats are fond of plaid shirts," Sara said. "And apparently they like corduroy, too. I'll have to keep that in mind. But what are you doing here, Dr. Williams? It's Saturday again. Are you determined to ruin every one of my weekends?"

"I'll tell you what I'm doing here," he snarled. He rummaged around in his pocket, helped along by Amaryllis, and pulled out a sheet of folded paper. Amaryllis promptly began to chew one corner.

"Hey—forget it, goat." Joshua yanked away the paper and stuck it under Sara's nose. "I found this on my desk this morning. Do you mind explaining it, Ms. Bennett?"

"Not at all. That's a copy of Employee Deposition Form 43-D. I filed it yesterday with the dean's office and left a copy last night where you'd be sure to find it. You found it. So what's the problem?"

"Ms. Bennett, it says here that you're lodging a grievance against me for—what the devil did you call it?" He scanned the form impatiently. "Here it is. It's a grievance against me for 'uncongeniality.' Is this some kind of crazed joke?"

"Absolutely not. You're trying to fire me for incompatibility. And I'm blocking that charge on the basis of uncongeniality. It's all according to college procedures. In case you didn't know, Employee Deposition 43-D has to be resolved before the outcome of Personnel Action Notice B-29 can be decided—''

''Lord, this is bureaucracy run amok. And you're part of it, Ms. Bennett!''

''I didn't want to be part of it. But you forced me. You didn't leave me any other choice.'' Sara bent to scratch Laddie behind the ears. The collie sat down, panting a little from the journey across the field. Sara was glad to see Laddie, but her reaction to seeing the dog's master was very mixed. Part of her was indignant that Joshua had invaded her farm. Another part of her was, quite simply, elated to see him here in his bright plaid shirt, his russet hair rumpled by the breeze—as if she didn't see enough of the aggravating man at the college.

The goats appeared to be jealous of her attentions to Laddie. Both of them left Joshua and crowded beside her. She scratched them behind the ears, too. They had lovely eyes, her goats—with a golden color that was almost translucent. And their eyes seemed to brim with a lighthearted wisdom, as if goats knew the true secrets of life.

''Yes, Daisy...yes, Amaryllis, I haven't forgotten about you,'' Sara murmured. ''Tomorrow I'll bring along some turnips for you to munch on.''

''What kind of names are those?'' Joshua asked. ''Are you telling me you actually called a goat Amaryllis?''

Sara straightened up. ''It's one of my favorite flowers, the amaryllis. So of course I'd call a goat that.''

Joshua surveyed the other goats who were poking their heads through the fence to get a look at him. ''Don't tell me they all have flower names.''

"The one with the white patch on her side, that's Lily. And that's Begonia, that's Violet and over there you can see Rose and Bluebell. And Snapdragon—"

"Okay. I get the idea."

"I put a lot of thought into what I call my goats," Sara said defensively. "And why shouldn't I? They're very important to me. When I'm accepted into the Farm Managers Program, I'm really going to expand my herd. I'm going to have an impressive dairy operation."

Now Joshua surveyed her small milking shed. "Hmmph," was all he had to offer, in a most skeptical tone. Sara was annoyed, certainly not a new reaction where Joshua Williams was concerned.

"All right, Dr. Williams, I've explained Form 43-D to you. By now you realize that I'm not going to sit quietly by while you try to fire me. I won't go down without a fight! But let's at least give each other a break on the weekends. This is the second Saturday in a row you've disrupted."

"No, Ms. Bennett. This time you did the disrupting. I was all ready to settle down with my dog for a pleasant morning's work at the office...and then I see this form planted on my desk like a call to war. You wanted me to see it right away so it would foul up *my* weekend."

"I didn't expect you to come out here to complain in person. I have my own work to do. Goodbye, Dr. Williams. We can continue this discussion on Monday." Sara hurried into the shed, grabbed two pails of milk and began hauling them toward the house. To her dismay, Joshua caught up to her and took the pails.

"Where do you want these?" he asked in a gruff voice.

"I can carry them myself. The last thing I need is for you to be—gallant. I mean, for crying out loud . . ."

"Just tell me where you want them."

It wasn't any use standing there arguing with the man. Sara knew how obstinate he could be. She proceeded to shoo Daisy and Amaryllis behind the fence with the other goats. She locked the gate firmly and doublechecked it; Daisy especially was notorious for unlocking gates. Then Sara began leading Joshua toward her house. The goats protested loudly to see her go. They made an awful noise, somewhere between a bleat and a wail, sounding as if they were being run over by a tractor. Sara tried to ignore them, but Joshua wouldn't let her.

"Do you enjoy having animals who howl like banshees?" he asked sardonically.

"I'm fond of goats, any way you look at it. They're intelligent and curious . . . and they're not afraid to express their emotions."

"Obviously not."

Progress toward the farmhouse was slow. Joshua walked at barely a turtle's pace so that Laddie could keep up. Sara marveled at the way Joshua could be so testy with *her* and yet so patient with his elderly dog. He was a man of contradictions and she wondered if she'd ever figure him out. But right now she didn't want to figure him out. She just wanted him gone!

At last they reached the cold room leading off Sara's kitchen. She took the pails from Joshua and poured the milk into one of the large cans resting in a water tank. Now the milk would cool to the proper temperature. She rinsed her pails at the sink in the corner.

"So this is what you're going to turn into a big dairy operation," Joshua said. He glanced around the small, bare room. Sara wished she didn't feel so defensive.

"It will be nothing like this when I'm in the Farm Managers Program. Eventually I'll be able to put up a whole new building ... Bennett's Dairy Farm, that's what it'll be. The goats will be almost more important than growing corn and beans and wheat."

"Sounds pretty ambitious."

"I have to be ambitious if I'm going to survive as a farmer. Growing crops isn't enough. I need to have something I can depend on even when the weather turns my beans moldy or rots my corn. Goats are the key. I'm already starting to get a reputation for my goat cheese—" Sara stopped herself. She was letting her enthusiasm get away from her, sharing her plans with Joshua. So far he'd done nothing but look around her farm with a judgmental air. What made her think she could share anything with him?

They left the cold room and Sara was relieved to be back out in the sun. The day was exceptionally warm for this Colorado autumn and she welcomed the clear skies after all that rain. She glanced down the drive at Joshua's shiny Jeep.

"Well, goodbye," she said. "Too bad you had to drive out here for nothing."

"It won't be for nothing, Ms. Bennett."

"What are you talking about?" she asked suspiciously, but he didn't answer. He'd gone back to being taciturn. And he made no move to leave. All he did was stand back to study her farmhouse. Sara studied it, too, wishing she could afford either the time or the money to whitewash the faded clapboards. But it was a good, sturdy house—a rambling two story built by her great-grandfather and added to by her grand-father. Unfortunately, the two men had held differing views of what a home should be and many of the de-tails didn't harmonize. The house was therefore like a lady adorned with garish furbelows that didn't suit her retiring personality. The original austerity of the house had been embellished with an exuberant bay window, a porch with rather alarming Grecian pillars and or-nate, unwieldy balustrades. But Sara loved every inch of it, no matter how startling, and she didn't like the critical way Joshua was examining the place.

"It's a very solid house," she declared. "Maybe a little original as to architectural design—but it's solid."

"Yeah, sure."

"Goodbye, Dr. Williams."

"I can't leave yet. You still haven't agreed to with-draw Form D-whatever."

"Employee Deposition Form 43-D. And I'll with-draw it the minute you withdraw Personnel Action Notice B-29."

"Can't be done. You're not suitable as my research assistant. Not suitable at all."

Sara curled her fingers against her palms. "Fine. But by the time all the committees have met and dis-cussed our problem, it'll be well into December. Christmastime, even. I'll have graduated—and I won't need your blasted job any more!"

"Clever, Ms. Bennett. I'll hand you that. You came up with a clever plan."

"I can defend myself when I have to. And you might as well admit when you're defeated. All you have to do is tolerate me a few more months. Is that so impossible?"

He stuffed his hands into the pockets of his trousers and began to pace back and forth in the yard. Laddie tried to pace with him and was beginning to pant again. Joshua stopped, apparently so his dog could have a rest.

"No...I can't tolerate you for even a few months," Joshua said finally. "A lot can happen in a few months—too much can happen, in fact."

"Was that the story with your other research assistant? She stayed on too long and that's how the trouble started?"

His face hardened. "I told you not to ask about that again. I can't discuss it with you."

Sara kicked at a stone with the toe of her work boot. "It's impossible to discuss anything with you. We'll just have to let the forms battle it out for us. Anyway, I have a lot to do today and I'd like to get started, so if you don't mind—"

"You don't like me being here, do you, Sara?"

She angled the brim of her cap more sharply over her forehead. "No, I don't like it one bit. But I guess you don't need a Ph.D. in biology to figure *that* out. It's only reasonable. You didn't like me poking around in your house and learning that you tap-danced when you were a kid. Well, I don't like you poking around out here and sneering at my goats."

Joshua rubbed his jaw, looking thoughtful. "Interesting," he said. "Very interesting."

"Dr. Williams, too bad I don't have time to stand around and chat about what you find so *very* interesting. But today's the first chance I've had to start combining. The weather's good for once and I can't waste it."

Joshua was looking more interested all the time. "Where are your workers? So far I haven't seen a single other person on this place."

"I don't use any hired labor. I don't need it. I'll work by myself this weekend. One of my neighbors will help me out during the week. Whenever he has a chance, he'll harvest for me while I'm at the college. Then I'll take over again in the evenings. It's a good system, so you don't need to act so—so darn scornful."

"I'm not scornful," Joshua answered slowly. "I'm . . . surprised. When you said you ran a farm, I didn't realize you meant singlehandedly. I didn't realize you were in such bad shape out here."

Sara stiffened. "Everything's in very good shape. I have it all under control—"

"Ms. Bennett, you don't have anything under control. Instead you're harboring grandiose dreams about turning a few rowdy goats into a major dairy operation. At the same time, you're under the delusion you can attend classes, work for me and still bring in an entire harvest with the sporadic help of a neighbor. Lord. If I'd realized any of this, I never would've accepted you in the first place. You don't have any business trying to do so much."

Sara folded her arms tightly. "I suppose this is another tactic to make me quit my job. Maybe you think I'll throw up my hands in defeat and tell you you're right—I just don't have the time to be your research assistant. Well, you're wrong. I won't give in. I'll show up every day for work and I'll go on being the best damn assistant you ever had. I'll do that all through harvest time. And I'll get such a good grade point average no *way* can the Farm Managers Program turn me down after I graduate. I'll do all that, Dr. Williams, and you won't be able to stop me!"

He shook his head. "It's difficult to believe anyone could be this foolish. Just tell me how you're going to manage it today, for instance. Are you planning to combine and haul your own grain, too?"

Sara moved into the shade of an ancient oak tree that guarded her house. She felt she needed some protection from Joshua. Damn him, he wouldn't let up. He was assailing her, exposing her biggest fear: that somehow she wouldn't be able to manage it all. In the middle of trying to keep her frantic schedule together, she might make one small misstep and everything would go toppling over like a row of dominoes. But she couldn't let Joshua see her fear.

"When I need a break from combining—yes, I'll haul my grain to the storage bins. It'll make for some variety."

"It'll make for some monumental inefficiency. You'll hardly get any work done. Looks like I'll have to step in." Joshua began rolling up the sleeves of his plaid shirt. "I'll run the combine for you today. You can haul the grain."

Sara stared at him. "What do you know about running a combine? It's darn tricky. It takes a lot of practice to do it right."

"I didn't learn about hybrid corn by sitting on my tailbone. I know farming, Ms. Bennett. What are you waiting for? Let's get to work."

She almost laughed. "You spend most of your time trying to fire me, but now you think you're going to help me bring in my harvest. I don't get it."

"Somebody has to save you from your own idiocy. Doesn't look like anybody else is around, so I'm elected."

Sara had gone beyond mere anger. All she wanted to do was holler at Dr. Joshua Williams. Somehow she managed to keep her voice cool and calm. "I've run this farm ever since my father died and I've done a good job of it. Okay, so maybe right now my schedule is a little more... packed than usual. But I sure as heck don't need to be rescued by anybody. Least of all by *you*, Dr. Williams. Good Lord, you're behaving as if you're a knight charging around on a white horse. Or in a combine, that is. But go be so all-fired chivalrous somewhere else!"

He merely went on rolling up his sleeves. "They're predicting more rain for this weekend. You can't afford to waste another minute."

Sara almost did start hollering now. Joshua's expression had turned stubborn—and it was a very familiar expression to her after working with him these past weeks. She knew from experience that once he made up his mind to do something, he wouldn't let anything—or anyone—stand in his way.

Sara wrapped the end of her braid around one hand and gave it a good, hard tug. Joshua Williams was possibly the most exasperating person she'd ever known. He wasn't just offering to help her. He was *insisting* on helping her. And he was doing it in such a way that she wanted to chase him out of the yard with a pitchfork. But in spite of the sunny weather, storm clouds were indeed threatening the horizon. Sara had run out of time to fight with Joshua.

"Oh, hell," she said. "Let's do it, then. Let's start the harvest!"

SARA SAT HIGH UP IN THE cab of the combine, wheeling the monstrous machine into her first cornfield. The combine truly was a monster, engine roaring hungrily in its bowels, picker snouts ready to swallow up ear after ear of corn. The combine would chew all that corn into red-gold grain and spew it out again through its long auger tube. Whenever Sara cranked the big steering wheel, she felt like she was subduing a beast, making the machine do her bidding and no one else's. It was a masterful, exhilarating sensation—but this morning it was marred by Joshua's intrusion on the farm. The man was trying to take over everything!

After he'd railroaded her into accepting his help, he'd insisted on being the one to man the combine. He and Sara had engaged in another prolonged and frustrating argument. Sara was determined to combine; after all, she had a lot more experience at it than Joshua, and she knew she could handle the machine best. She'd finally won...by rule of possession. She'd clambered up the ladder into the cab and driven the machine out of the old barn where she kept it stored. That had left Joshua with no choice but to be in charge of the tractor and grain wagons.

Now Sara rumbled along the first rows of cornstalks, feeding the combine those ears of beautiful yellow kernels. She worked expertly, knowing from long practice when to adjust the control levers. She wondered how much of a hindrance Joshua's help was actually going to be. It was easy enough for him to say he knew farming, but how would that translate into actual work? This day might turn into a disaster, for all Sara could tell. She began to envy Laddie, shut away in the house. Laddie had whined at being left behind, protesting almost as much as the goats had. But at least the collie wouldn't have to witness any more arguments between Sara and Joshua.

Sara made her way around the outside of the field, laying the groundwork so that later she could make smooth passes up and down the middle of the field. Then she saw Joshua coming toward her on the tractor, hauling a grain wagon behind him. He looked good on a tractor. He looked better than good, riding the machine high and easy as if he'd been born to a farm. His red hair had turned fiery in the sun. Sara gazed at him, bewildered by the rush of longing that swept through her. But what did she long for? Not Joshua Williams—surely not Joshua...

And that was when it happened. Because she was gazing at Joshua, Sara didn't watch what she was doing. Quick as anything, the picker head dug into a mound of earth and started eating dirt instead of corn. Sara brought the combine to a bumpy halt, but already it was too late. The picker was clogged.

Face burning in mortification, Sara scrambled out of the cab. She knelt in front of the picker, pulled on her work gloves and began scooping out the dirt. She prayed that Joshua would mind his own business, but that was too much to hope for. He swung down from the tractor and came strolling over to her.

"Having problems?"

"Nothing I can't solve on my own."

"Thought you said you knew how to handle this thing, Ms. Bennett. That was a beginner's mistake."

"It was a mistake, all right. If I hadn't been watching you—if you hadn't barged your way onto my farm in the first place—" Sara couldn't even talk straight any more. A blush seemed to be heating up her entire body. She wasn't about to tell Joshua that ogling him had included some heartfelt admiration on her part. She went on scrabbling away at the dirt in the picker throat. Joshua knelt beside her.

"That stuff's really packed in there," he said. "You'll never get it clear like that."

"Listen, Dr. Williams, I *do* know combines. Leave this to me and find something else to do. Go ride around on the tractor some more, why don't you?" But that wasn't a good suggestion. Joshua riding around on a tractor was what had got Sara into trouble in the first place.

"Do you have a toolbox anywhere?" he asked.

"In the cab. But—"

Joshua was already climbing into the machine. He reappeared a few moments later, wielding a crowbar. "This'll do the job. It'll loosen up that dirt." He knelt beside Sara again and pushed the end of the crowbar into the stubbornly wedged dirt. Sara sat up, resting her gloved hands on her knees.

"Do you always need to be in charge of everything?" she demanded.

"Yeah. Pretty much like you need to prove you can do everything on your own, without any help."

"I'm not like that. I'm willing to accept help. It's just *your* help I'm concerned about."

Joshua gave her a thoughtful look. "No... you really do want to do everything on this farm yourself. It seems to be a matter of pride with you. What are you really trying to prove, Sara? That you're strong and self-sufficient? That you don't need anybody else? What, exactly?"

She took off one of her gloves and slapped it against her leg. "For somebody who can't talk about himself, you sure seem to be having an enjoyable time discussing *me*. Well, stop. You don't know what I'm like."

He continued working imperturbably with his crowbar. "I'm starting to get a pretty fair picture. Here it is. You accuse me of not admitting any weaknesses in myself. But you're just as bad. You won't admit you have any limitations. You think you should be able to handle school, a job and a farm all on your own. As I said, it seems to be a point of pride with you."

Sara yanked off her other glove. "I don't have any choice but to handle school and my job and the farm. It doesn't have anything to do with pride."

He chuckled. "That word really bothers you, doesn't it? Makes you touchy."

Sara had never seen Joshua Williams in such a good mood...a good mood at her expense. With her bare hands she started rooting out more dirt from the picker. It was very irksome to see that Joshua was making most of the progress. Using his crowbar, he soon had the picker throat clear and ready to swallow corn again.

"There. You can start her up," he said in a tone of great satisfaction. "Aren't you glad I was here to get you out of this jam, Ms. Bennett?" Humor sparkled in his eyes. Imagine that. Joshua Williams was actually mirthful—and all because he was succeeding in provoking Sara no end.

She scrambled to her feet and glared at him. "Out of my way, Dr. Williams. Because now...now I'm going to show you what combining is *really* about!"

CHAPTER SEVEN

SARA FINISHED HARVESTING the field without one further glitch. She was proud of her accomplishment—until she remembered that Joshua had accused her of being proud, of needing to prove something. His words rankled. She wanted to forget what he'd said, but she didn't seem able to do that.

She dumped her load of corn into the wagon. Sara could store only so much of the harvest on her land; eventually she'd have to resort to the grain elevators in town. But it felt good to know that the first corn of the season would be stowed snugly on her own farm. She planned to hold off selling most of her crop as long as she could, waiting for better prices on grain. It was all part of the precarious juggling act she had to perform constantly with her finances.

Before she took the combine to another field, she watched Joshua hauling the wagon over to the storage bins. He was as powerful and self-assured as any farmer she'd known. By now Sara was learning that he possessed a myriad of talents. He was a brilliant scientist, a caring teacher... and a tap dancer to boot. Today she was forced to add that he was also a competent farmer. She decided it was much more gratifying when she could find fault with the man.

She didn't have any such gratification the rest of the day. Joshua worked right alongside her, tireless and efficient. In the afternoon, when it was time for her to milk the goats again, he took over the combine. And he turned out to be good with the machine, hang it all. He could go through a field and pick it clean and neat, then move on to the next. When he'd said he knew how to farm, he hadn't been exaggerating.

The first raindrops began to fall at dusk, forcing Sara and Joshua to quit for the day. They barely had the machinery back in the barn before the downpour really began. Sara ran across the yard toward the house, Joshua right behind her. Her feet slithered a little in the mud and he caught hold of her. They'd been a team today, no way could Sara get around that. They'd worked well together. And for the first time they'd worked as equals, not as professor and research assistant. Hadn't that brought a subtle change to their relationship? If anything, perhaps it had added a certain awkwardness.

Together they stood in the shelter of the porch, watching the rain, not speaking. Sara didn't look at Joshua, but she was intensely aware of him. And somehow that made her more intensely aware of the beauty around her—the fertile beauty of her farm. The fields were shrouded in wet gloom, but the memory of sunshine lingered. A last glimmer of daylight was reflected on the pond where wild geese came to flock. The rain softened the graying wood of the sheds and barns; it muted the stark outlines of the trees along the drive. In the rain, the past and future of the farm seemed to blur together: all the years of struggle, the promise of prosperity just ahead. At last Sara had to speak, trying to share a hint of what she saw and felt.

"There's something special about the first day of harvest. Makes you realize how alive a farm is. I mean, the soil's alive, and so is every single kernel of corn. You can feel the life of it all, just by getting dirt under your fingernails. Makes you happy...makes *me* happy, anyway. All in all, I think we had a very good day."

Joshua shook his head. "In terms of practicality, it was a lousy day's work. No farm should be operated like this. Hardly any manpower, not enough equipment...at this rate, maybe you'll get the harvest in by the time you're ninety-two."

With only a few words, he'd managed to destroy Sara's mellow contentment. All her worries returned full force. How would she keep her grain moisture down in this damp weather? How would she deal with the disturbing new rattle the combine had developed this afternoon? How would she ever salvage her beans if it kept raining like this? Oh, curse Joshua Williams for bringing it all back to her!

"Look, I know this farm needs a lot of improvement. That's the whole point of getting in with the Farm Managers Program. But for right now, to-day...we did start the harvest. And in spite of all the problems, I have the privilege of farming land that's been in my family for over a hundred years. Think about that! It'll send shivers up your spine."

"The only thing sending shivers up my spine is the corn chaff down my shirt. Ms. Bennett, you need to quit dreaming about your quaint family farm and face the way things really are."

She swiveled around to confront him squarely. "Okay—tell me. Just how are things, really?"

"You're in way over your head with this place. And you're gambling that one single program, the Farm Managers, can pull you out of trouble. What if you're not accepted into the program? What then?"

She stared at him in the deepening twilight. "I *will* be accepted. I won't allow any other possibility."

He shook his head again. "I hate to see you heading for a fall, Sara. Dammit... I do hate to see that." He sounded almost surprised by his own concern. But Sara figured she could do without concern like Joshua's.

"You know what I want in my life?" she said. "Someone who'll cheer me on, encourage my dreams. Not someone like you who has to point out all the problems and make them sound even worse than they are. That I don't need."

"Too bad. Someone realistic like me might actually help you save your farm."

"I'm saving the farm just fine on my own."

"Garbage. You need help. And you need it well before you're eligible for that Farm Managers thing."

"Whatever I need, it's not *you*, Joshua. And in case you forgot, you seem to feel the same way about me. You're trying to fire me, after all."

"I'm not forgetting that," he grumbled. "No way am I forgetting that."

"Well, then. I guess we know where we stand with each other."

"Right. That much is pretty damn clear."

There didn't seem to be anything more to say. Laddie was scratching at the other side of the front door, so Sara swung it open and the old collie hobbled out joyfully to greet his master. Joshua offered no greeting in return, but his rigid stance seemed to relax a little. Seeing Joshua with his dog had an odd effect on Sara. She found herself saying something completely unexpected; she listened to her own words with dismay.

"You must be starving. I didn't even feed you lunch. And—well, believe it or not, I *am* grateful for what you did today. Let me repay you with a home-cooked supper."

"No payment necessary."

"It really would make me feel better if I did something for you. I'm a good cook."

He hesitated, obviously wanting to turn her down. Sara couldn't understand why she didn't just let him go. This morning all she'd tried to do was get him off the farm. What was wrong with her now—why did she want so badly for him to stay?

"It can't hurt to eat one meal under my roof," she said. "The rumors about us have already started. One supper, more or less...what difference can it make?"

"I *am* hungry," he admitted, but in a doubtful manner. "Work like that really stirs up an appetite." He considered her offer another moment, finally giving a brusque nod. "I'll eat and then I'm out of here. Any place I can wash up?"

"Down the hall, two doors to your right. I'll just go clean off a little myself." Once inside the house, Sara hurried up the creaking staircase, wondering what she'd let herself in for with her impromptu supper invitation. She'd be sorry for it, sure as anything. Joshua was even more irksome out here than he was at the college. He was so damn clinical in analyzing her farm. He didn't understand that farming had to be about dreaming as much as about anything else. Who but a dreamer would gamble every day with fickle weather and fluctuating crop prices and land values you could never really count on? Without dreams, a farm would be sterile; it wouldn't thrive. That was what Sara believed and she didn't need Joshua Williams undermining her confidence. So why the heck had she invited him to supper? All her common sense where he was concerned seemed to have vanished!

She took a quick shower in the upstairs bathroom, the ancient pipes clanging. It was strange how the noise of the pipes could be an intimate sound—all because Joshua was in the house. Sara dried off as fast as she could, unbraided her hair and tried to brush out all the dust and grime from the day's work. It was a futile task; what she really needed was to wash her hair. But she didn't have time for that....

Goodness, she was concerned about primping for Joshua—the man who'd already accused her of being too pretty. He'd probably be more than happy if she went downstairs with her hair in a bun and her body disguised in a feed sack. Sara left her hair loose, refusing to brush out even one more snarl. Wrapped in her frayed flannel robe, she strode from the bathroom to her bedroom. The floorboards screaked under her feet, announcing her progress. This house was talkative, a fact she welcomed when she was alone. It gave her a sense of company. But with Joshua downstairs, she'd prefer silence. She didn't want the house telling any of her secrets. After all, Joshua didn't want to share any of his secrets with *her*.

In the bedroom she rifled through her closet, wishing that the selection would have magically improved since the last time she looked. If anything, her wardrobe was sparser than ever; she hadn't had time lately even to do the wash. She was reduced to a summer dress in a cotton print. But it was an attractive dress, with a scooped neckline and small pearl buttons all down the front. The skirt belled out gently from the trim waistline. Sara struggled with the tiny buttons, trying to do them up too fast and getting her thumb stuck in a buttonhole. She could almost sense Joshua's impatience rising through the floorboards like an ominous rain cloud that had invaded the house. He'd made it clear that all he wanted to do was eat and then leave. Fine. That was what she wanted, too. She'd slap some food in front of him and then hustle him out the door!

At last she was finished with her buttons. She slipped on her faithful buckaroo boots, turning her dress into a country girl's outfit. She dabbed on some perfume that she hadn't worn in over a year, tossed back her tangled ripple of hair and marched down to Joshua. Her boot heels made a defiant tap against the wooden stairs.

Joshua stood by the front door, as if debating whether or not to make his escape right now. He examined Sara with the same critical air he had used to survey her goats. Sara waited for him to pronounce judgment, but he offered nothing beyond a skeptical "Hmm." The reaction she got from Laddie was more enthusiastic; the collie wagged his long, plumed tail when he saw her.

Joshua's eyes seemed darker than usual and he went on gazing at Sara, frowning slightly. She rubbed her arms, wishing that instead of this summery dress she'd seen fit to wear jeans and one of her baggy sweaters. Wouldn't she ever learn that dressing up for Joshua got her nowhere?

Wait a minute. She was behaving as if she *wanted* to get somewhere with Joshua. He was a grouchy, demanding man who never expressed appreciation for her work, who was determined to fire her and who scoffed at her dreams even while helping her to bring in the harvest. And yet, in spite of all this, Sara found herself behaving as if she actually had romantic notions about him. She was behaving as if that "nudge" in the conservatory hadn't merely been an accident.

Appalled at herself, Sara brushed past Joshua and fled to the kitchen. Why had she offered to feed him— why? She yanked open the door of the refrigerator and stared inside. She saw some speckled eggs from her neighbor's chickens, a hunk of goat cheese, a few cartons of yogurt, a few carrots, some limp spinach and several apples so ripe they were starting to pucker. She *was* a good cook...when she had the time. Imaginative dealings with food had become one more luxury she'd sacrificed.

Joshua and Laddie followed her into the kitchen. Joshua sat down at the table and Laddie plopped beside him. Sara glanced at the two of them. She still had a chance to retract her supper invitation. But Joshua wore the beleaguered expression of someone submitting to torture. That was enough to make Sara go through with inflicting it. He'd accepted her invitation and they would both see it through to the end.

"I'll have something whipped up in a jiffy," she said, hauling out the entire contents of the refrigerator and dumping everything on the counter. As she began shredding the limp carrots, Joshua drummed his fingers on the tabletop.

"This place is a throwback to the 1950s," he said. "Or to the 1890s, I can't decide which."

"It's some of both. The appliances are only about forty years old, but that hearthstone dates from the turn of the century. Over there on the shelf, that's Great-grandma Bennett's collection of crockery. And hanging from the ceiling beams, those are her original laundry baskets."

"Lord. Do you keep everything that ever belonged to your family?"

"If it's still useful—you bet. Nothing goes to waste on this farm, absolutely nothing." It was more than that, of course. Sara harbored a strong streak of nostalgia where her family was concerned. She couldn't bear to part with any of the heirlooms that had been handed down to her. And so she retained items that were questionable, to say the least. For example, all the chairs here in the kitchen were adorned with the fussy cushions Great-aunt Lucy had sewn by hand. They were truly awful cushions, with little ruffled skirts that made the chair legs look like the limbs of spindly schoolgirls. And Sara couldn't honestly say she cared for Uncle Howell's murky painting of cows in a field, but she left it hanging over the kitchen mantel as a tribute to her uncle's dubious artistic talent. She believed that any and all family history should be faithfully preserved; she saw herself in a way as the family curator and archivist. And if that made her house into an odd sort of Bennett museum—she was happy with that.

As rain spattered against the windowpanes, a meal began to take shape under Sara's hands. The spinach looked a good deal fresher once she'd washed and chopped it for a salad; the apples were sweet with their ripeness and she chopped them up, too. Spinach, apples, carrots, all tossed together in a crystal punch bowl that had once belonged to Grandma Bennett—Sara couldn't have asked for a more festive salad. Yogurt and crumbled goat cheese made an impromptu dressing and Sara added a lot of cheese to the eggs she scrambled up. Now the only problem was finding something to drink. She popped down to the cellar and unearthed one of Grandpa Bennett's vintage wines. Once in the kitchen again, she dusted off the bottle and uncorked it. Joshua gave the bottle a distrustful inspection.

"It's the very best," Sara told him. "My grandfather believed that any country estate should have a stock of wine. He was a connoisseur. All we have to do is let it breathe a little."

"That stuff looks so grizzled it'll probably need CPR to breathe."

Sara decided to ignore this remark. She set a plate of scrambled eggs in front of Joshua. Then, in spite of his disapproving stare, she resurrected a dog dish from the cabinet under the sink and gave Laddie a serving of scrambled eggs, too.

Sara settled in front of her own eggs at the beechwood table. "It feels good to have a dog around here again. When I'm in with the Farm Managers, I'll have the time to get myself a dog." She pushed a plate of sliced cheese toward Joshua. "Here, have some more of this. It's from my own goats, you know. You won't find better goat cheese anywhere."

Joshua had been eating his salad and eggs with apparent gusto, but now he stopped. "That's what you put in all this stuff—goat cheese!"

"Of course. And you're enjoying it, I know you are. Why can't you finally admit I'm doing something right on my farm?"

Joshua prodded his eggs with his fork. He glanced down at Laddie, who'd already licked his dish clean. Shrugging a little, Joshua went on eating. "Not too bad," he said grudgingly after a moment. Sara wondered if she should take this as a compliment for her cooking; she wasn't likely to get any other. She poured Joshua a glass of the red wine and he sipped it. She sipped from her own glass, savoring the rich, fruity taste. It reminded her of the ripe autumn apples she'd tossed into the salad. This was a harvest wine, worthy to celebrate the season. Sara lifted her glass in a toast.

"Here's to reaping and gleaning." Her mind's eye reached into the past, imagining sickles and scythes, their blades glinting in the sun as they were wielded by her ancestors. But Joshua didn't seem to capture her vision. He didn't even complete the toast. He did nothing but give her a sour look over the rim of his glass.

Sara jumped up and went to put the kettle on. She was annoyed enough with Joshua that she needed a strong tea tonight: rosemary or perhaps even marjoram. She stood at the stove with her back to Joshua, knowing that now was the time to tell him good-night,

to get him out of her house. But once again she said
something she didn't expect to say.

"It's chilly...I'll build a fire for us in the living
room. We can take our wine and tea in there."

Joshua was constantly surprising her. He didn't argue. He didn't hesitate. He simply picked up Grandpa
Bennett's bottle of wine and the two half-empty
glasses. Together he and Laddie made their way slowly
but steadily into the living room. Sara raised her eyebrows.

"Well, what do you know about that," she murmured to herself. A few moments later she followed
man and dog, balancing her tea tray.

She made the fire quickly, expertly, the way she had
to do everything these days if she was going to keep
her life on track. Only a few logs remained in the box
by the hearth, which meant more money for fire-
wood...she suppressed the thought. If she continued
this way, always adding and subtracting the figures of
her meager budget, her brain would turn into a cal-
culator.

The fire crackled cheerfully. Sara pulled an overstuffed armchair close to it and sat down. Joshua sat
across from her on the other side of the coffee table,
reclining in his own overstuffed chair. He seemed to be
having difficulty getting comfortable, shifting around
as if ants were crawling up his socks.

"These are dreadfully uncomfortable chairs," Sara
remarked. "Even Grandpa Bennett could never get
used to them and he was the one who insisted on
having them. They were part of his scheme for creating a country estate. He hired an interior decorator
and listened to absolutely every word she said." Sara

gestured at the ornate marble chimneypiece, the gilded wood molding, the flocked wallpaper thick as velvet. "The decorator said Grandpa should aim for a style of 'relaxed elegance,' and this is how it turned out. Heavy on the elegance, but not a whole lot of relaxation. It's too bad the decorator got all the money that should've gone into farm equipment."

"Lord. Has everybody in your family been an impractical dreamer?"

Sara took a hearty swallow of marjoram tea, but it didn't make her any less annoyed at Joshua. "Maybe my grandfather was impractical. And my father, too. He got the place far too much into debt. Contrary to your opinion, though, *I'm* not impractical. I know exactly what needs to be done to turn the farm around. And I'm going to do it once I'm—"

"Once you're in the Farm Managers Program," Joshua finished for her, his tone dry. "I know. That's when everything will be perfect. That's when you'll be in farm utopia."

Sara bit back a retort and drank some more tea. No sense in upsetting Laddie; the old dog seemed particularly sensitive to emotion. He would prick up his ears in worried fashion when Joshua and Sara talked, as if sensing the undercurrents between them. Now, as a silence stretched out, he rested his head on his paws, still looking faintly anxious. Sara reached down to pet him. He wagged his tail for her and at last closed his eyes. After a moment he began to snore. It was a comfortable sound, easing the tension, providing an excuse for companionable silence. Because the silence *was* companionable, no doubt about it. That surprised Sara as much as anything tonight, but she welcomed this unexpected camaraderie with the man who usually aggravated her more than anyone in the world.

Joshua finally seemed to have found a semitolerable position in the overstuffed chair. He was slouched down a little, one ankle resting on his knee. Sara noted that today his socks matched. They were argyle socks in bright yellow and blue and green. Sara poured another cup of tea and offered it to Joshua.

"Try some of this. Marjoram is very soothing. For once you seem to be relaxed, but you can't be too sure how long it'll last. Drink some tea, and maybe you can prolong the mood."

His mouth twitched; it was almost a smile. "If you knew me better, Ms. Bennett, you'd realize I'm really a sociable guy."

"Could've fooled me. But have some tea. It'll do you good."

He picked up the cup and sniffed it. Then he coughed. "What is this stuff? Smells like it could strip varnish."

"It's my own special formula. Go ahead—drink it. You force your poor research plants to drink all sorts of concoctions. You ought to find out just what it's like."

His mouth twitched again. Yes, that was definitely a ghost of a smile. Extraordinary; she and Dr. Joshua Williams were sharing a joke of sorts together. At the sound of their voices, Laddie had opened his eyes again, but this time he didn't look worried. After a second or two he drifted back off to sleep.

Joshua took a cautious sip of tea and grimaced. He reached for his wineglass. "I think I'd better wash down that...concoction. Where did you learn to brew stuff like that?''

"My mother was the one who started me on teas— all kinds. Whenever I was tired, she'd give me goldenrod tea. If I had a stomachache, it was bee balm. And if I wasn't sick at all—if we were just sitting at the table for a good talk after I got home from school— then she'd give me orange mint or lavender tea.'' Sara's fingers tightened on her cup. She hadn't meant to start remembering her mother. Usually she was too busy to remember, always rushing between classes, her job and the farm. But now, sitting here quietly next to Joshua, listening to the mild rumble of Laddie's snore, memories of her parents crowded in on her.

"What happened to your mother? Where is she now?'' Joshua asked in a low voice. She glanced at him sharply, wondering if she could trust this new gentleness in him. The lines of his face seemed to have softened, but perhaps that was only an illusion created by the play of firelight over his features. Nonetheless, Sara answered his question. She allowed her memories to take over.

"The winter I turned eighteen, my mother had a stroke and simply never recovered. She died that spring. She was already sixty—both she and my father were in their forties when I was born. Anyway, after she died, my dad seemed lost somehow. He died a few years later himself. Emphysema, that was the official cause, but I think it was a broken heart as much as anything else. He just didn't know how to live without my mother. They were crazy about each other. Sometimes it embarrassed me, the way they'd hold hands and kiss all the time. But I guess deep down I was pleased that my parents were so in love. It made them special.'' Sara stopped herself, aware that she was rambling too much. Joshua, who'd never known her parents, could probably care less about their love story. But his expression appeared to be one of genuine interest. He drank his wine, not saying anything—and his very silence seemed to be an invitation for Sara to go on.

She stirred her marjoram tea. ''You'd think that having older parents like that would've been dull. But it wasn't, not in the least. Both my father and mother were always laughing and joking around, always deciding at the last minute that it was time for the three of us to go to a movie. Or maybe it would be ice-skating, or swimming if it was summer. We'd swim in the pond and leave all the farm work for later. Anyway, I miss them. I wish they'd both lived to be ninety-five, smooching away and teasing each other and embarrassing me. I try to keep the farm going in their memory...but I'd give anything just to have them back again.''

Sara held onto her cup, blinking rapidly, mortified at her sudden tears. She believed that crying was natural and healthy, that it was good to weep and get out emotions whenever necessary, but she darn well didn't want to do it in front of Joshua Williams. She had a suspicion he would say that crying was silly and weak minded. Already he seemed to be growing uncomfortable, as if he was sorry he'd encouraged her to talk. He shifted in his chair and glanced around. With an air of relief he picked up a book from the coffee table and concentrated on it.

"Thackeray's *Vanity Fair* ... I remember slogging through this in college, all seven hundred pages or so. Are you reading it for a class?"

His effort to change the subject was so obvious that Sara had to laugh. Her laughter came out rather choked. But after reminiscing about her parents she knew, quite suddenly and clearly, that they would have seen the humor in this situation, too. They would have joked and teased Joshua, poking fun at his reserved nature in a kindhearted way. That made Sara feel immensely better.

"No, I'm not reading *Vanity Fair* for a class. It's solely for pleasure. I love wonderful big books like that, even though it takes me forever to get through them. I keep telling myself that someday I'll have a whole afternoon to sit back, prop up my feet and read just for the fun of it. And someday I will."

"Right ... when everything's perfect—when you're in the Farm Managers Program. Then you'll have time to read seven hundred pages." Joshua set the book back on the table. He cleared his throat, tapped his fingers on the arm of his chair, gazed with a frown at his watch. Sara expected he was ready to jump out of his chair and head for the front door with his sleepy dog in tow.

But Joshua surprised her yet again. He stayed right where he was. He sat up straighter in the overstuffed armchair and stared at Sara as if she were some new strand of DNA he was struggling to unravel.

"All right, Ms. Bennett," he said. "I've been here on your farm all day. I've watched you, I've listened to you. I've seen a lot—just about everything I need to see. I've tried to keep my mouth shut, but I can't any longer. It's time for me to tell you exactly what your problem is. Lord, it sure as hell is time for *somebody* to tell you what your problem is. I don't want the job, but it looks like nobody else will do you the favor. So... here goes."

CHAPTER EIGHT

Sara stared at Joshua as the firelight guttered and then flared up again. "Forget my problem. You know what *your* problem is? You don't know how to keep your mouth shut. You've done nothing but criticize me since the moment we met. Well, that's it. I've had it. I don't need any more of your complaints. Do me a favor and keep your comments to yourself."

"I'm not going to criticize you. Instead, I'm going to give you some much-needed advice." Joshua had that stubborn look on his face that Sara already knew too well. Meanwhile, Laddie had woken up and was glancing with a troubled expression from Joshua to Sara and back again.

"At least think about your dog," Sara said. "Laddie can't bear it when we argue. It makes him nervous and unhappy. Have some consideration."

Joshua seemed a little startled by her words. He gazed at his collie. But then he shook his head. "Ms. Bennett, spare me your half-baked theories about canine psychology. If Laddie seems perturbed right now, it's probably because he has indigestion from eating goat cheese." Joshua rose and stood in front of Sara as if he were lecturing a student.

"You're going to listen to what I have to say," he told her grimly. "You need to hear it. Number one, you're hanging on to this farm in some futile attempt to enshrine your parents' memory. Not to mention the memory of your grandfather and his misguided architectural eccentricities. Number two, you're totally unwilling to accept your own limitations. For some reason I can't yet fathom, you feel you have to do all the work on the farm yourself. Maybe you believe that's the only way you can live up to your parents' legacy. Or maybe you're convinced that no one else in the whole world can measure up to your standards—who knows. And, number three—"

"I refuse to listen to number three," Sara declared. "Numbers one and two were more than enough." She struggled out of the overstuffed chair, needing to confront Joshua on an equal level. But he was still able to maintain the demeanor of a professor lecturing a student.

"Number three is the most important item of all, Ms. Bennett. And here it is. You've set up absurd, unrealistic expectations for this Farm Managers Program. I don't care how good the program is, no way can it match your expectations. By counting on it to solve all your problems, you're guaranteeing yourself a big disappointment."

Sara's indignation had reached the flammable stage. She felt like that fire crackling in her grate, with sparks flying up the chimney. She was ready to set off her own sparks, but she also knew that emotion wouldn't help her beat Joshua Williams. She had to remain as coolly logical as he was in order to win this argument and prove him one-hundred-percent wrong.

"You may not realize this, Dr. Williams, but I investigated the Farm Managers Program thoroughly before applying. I ascertained that it was my best chance for modernizing the farm—and yes, perhaps my only chance. The particular problems of my farm don't qualify me for any other programs I'm aware of." She took a deep breath and went on.

"Furthermore, when applying to the program, I drew up a detailed financial analysis of projected improvements, not to mention a ten-year crop-rotation schedule *and* a soil-conservation plan." Sara marched over to Grandpa Bennett's rolltop desk, grabbed a stack of papers and strode back to Joshua. "Here! It's all here. My proposal for the goat dairy, my outline for purchases of another more efficient combine, an electronic planter and brand-new chisel and disk systems. What more do you want?" Sara thrust her pile of papers toward Joshua, but he didn't take them. Instead he merely stood there, gazing at her with an expression that was unmistakable even in the erratic light of the fire. It was an expression of pity.

That undid Sara. To hell with reasoned discussions and cool explanations. She tossed all her plans, proposals and projections down on the coffee table. Then she faced Joshua defiantly.

"Okay, maybe I am a crazy dreamer. Maybe the odds are against me, no matter how many plans I make. But I'll keep on trying. I'm proud that I can honor my parents' legacy and keep this farm alive. I'm doing it for them and I'm doing it for myself."

"If you really want to do something for yourself, this is my advice. Sell the farm while you can still get something for it. Sell it before it takes you down. Don't hold on to it just out of this damn sentiment of yours."

"'Damn sentiment' is everything to me, Dr. Williams. I couldn't live without it. How can *you* live without it? How can you be so—so provokingly scientific all the time?"

Joshua, looking disgruntled, was silent. Laddie wagged his tail uncertainly. The only sounds were the hiss of the fire and the patter of rain on the roof. Shadows enveloped the room, cold and mysterious. Sara shivered and moved closer to the hearth until the heat of the fire burned the backs of her legs. At last Joshua spoke.

"Ms. Bennett, I happen to like being scientific and whatever else you want to call it—practical, unsentimental. And I'll tell you why. I grew up in a family that was nothing short of histrionic. I have a mother who went into fits of agony whenever she couldn't hit the right note on her violin. I have a father who acted out the tragedies of Shakespeare for unsuspecting and unwilling customers in his drugstore. Not to mention that both my parents were determined to turn all three of their children into melodramatic Broadway performers. The point is—"

"I understand now," Sara broke in eagerly. "That's why you were tap-dancing in those photographs. And playing the violin when you were a kid, even though you looked like you'd rather be bashing someone with it. This is fascinating."

He scowled at her. "My purpose isn't to entertain you with stories about the loony Williams family. I'm simply trying to illustrate a point. I know from experience how damaging excessive emotionality can be. Making decisions based on emotion is harmful for everyone affected by that decision. My parents, along with everything else they did, made an emotional decision to get divorced. They made an equally emotional decision to get back together again. Each time it was like putting their children on a roller coaster and throwing the switch.''

"You keep saying 'their children,''' Sara murmured. "You can't even talk about how all this affected *you*, Joshua. And that's what's truly damaging. Not being able to express your own emotions."

"I've heard that meaningless phrase too many times," Joshua said in a tone of deep disgust. "My mother likes to say it, my father likes to say it. Unfortunately, even my sisters like to say it. 'Express your emotions,' that's their motto. And they're all basket cases because of it."

"Even if you never say how you're feeling—the feelings are still there," Sara insisted. "I think you're a whole lot more sentimental than you let on. Why else would you keep that scrapbook with those photographs of you and your family?"

"Ms. Bennett, I keep that scrapbook for one purpose. To remind myself of what I *don't* want to be like. To remind myself what I won't ever become. But this conversation isn't about me. It's supposed to be about you."

"Maybe it's about us." Sara felt reckless, as if her anger at Joshua had fueled something rash and impulsive in her. She took a step toward him. "All these complaints you have about me, about the way I do things, about how I'm too emotional—maybe it's just a way for you to avoid the real issue between us."

"Lord, I've heard that one before, too," Joshua muttered. "My father always talks about getting to the

real issue, like someone digging through layers of dirty
clothes for a clean shirt.''

"You know what's really bothering you, Dr. Williams? It's the fact that I make you feel all sorts of
messy emotions. I'm your research assistant and yet
you want to kiss me. Around me you're experiencing
feelings you'd rather keep squashed down somewhere. Hah. You can't keep your feelings squashed
forever.''

"How do you know what you make me feel, Sara?''
His voice was tight, his eyes a dark, cindery gray in the
dim light. Sara tried to hold on to her own brashness,
but it was slipping away from her. Now she took a step
back from Joshua.

"Maybe I only know how I feel," she said.
"Hell . . . maybe I don't even know that. I don't suppose it will get us anywhere, anyway. You refuse to
understand why I'm fighting so hard for this farm.
And no matter what you feel about me . . . you'll
probably just keep saying I'm your research assistant
and you can't get involved.''

Joshua ran a hand through his corn-dusted hair and
now he looked tired. "Maybe I don't emote the way
you'd like, but I can sure tell you how I feel about you,
Ms. Bennett. You drive me nuts. You talk to plants,
you name goats after flowers. You accuse my dog of
being neurotic. And you've enshrined this pathetic
farm like it's some kind of monument. Yep, everything you do drives me nuts. It drives me crazy!''

Sara turned and poked at the fire, churning it up to
a fury of flames. "Dr. Williams, you know how to
express some emotions very well. Maybe too well.''
She clattered her poker down on the bricks before the

hearth. Then she turned to face Joshua again. She was exasperated with herself for still wanting to be close to him . . . for still wanting his kiss. Oh, but if she could just have one honest-to-goodness kiss from him! Not just a nudge this time. No, it would have to be a full-fledged kiss. And afterward she could tell herself it was over, that she'd had a genuine taste of his lips and could get on with thinking about other things.

Right now, however, she couldn't seem to think about anything but the possibility of Joshua's mouth touching hers. They were standing closer than before, staring at each other. After his day's work, Joshua smelled of the farm—of rich clean soil, of ripened corn and country rain. She breathed in deeply, wishing she could bury her face against Joshua's dusty shirt. His features were strained, his eyes darker than ever. He reached up a hand, brushing his fingers against her tangled hair. Sara felt her breath tremble. She ached for more from Joshua, but he dropped his hand abruptly.

"No," he said. "Dammit, I'm not going to do this."

"No . . ." Sara echoed on a sigh, although she couldn't keep the hope from her voice. It turned out to be useless hope. Joshua uttered one final oath and then he was gone, striding from her house. Laddie limped after him. The collie's attention was solely on reaching his master—no attention left for Sara now. And after a few moments the front door slammed. Both the professor and his dog had left her alone.

Sara sank back into her chair and gazed into the fire. Her face was hot, flushed, but the rest of her was cold. She draped her hair over her bare arms like a cloak, but that didn't help. The rambling old house was suddenly too big and drafty, too empty. At last Sara understood why she'd tried so hard to make Joshua linger tonight. She understood why she'd plied him with goat cheese, her grandfather's vintage wine and her mother's marjoram tea. She'd done it all because he'd chased away the emptiness in this house. He'd chased away the loneliness that had been growing here ever since her parents' deaths. And now, with Joshua gone, the loneliness had returned full force. It was back, worse than ever.

"I can't let him do this to me," she exclaimed out loud to the fire. "I can't be vulnerable to him." But saying the words did no good. She *was* vulnerable to him. He scoffed at her dreams, he denigrated all her emotions...and yet she was terribly lonely without him. What on earth was she going to do?

She sat by the fireplace until the last flames flickered down and only embers were left, glowing like the eyes of some dark creature. Sara poked at the embers, waiting for an answer to come to her. But no answer came in the rainy night...no solution at all to the enigma of Dr. Joshua Williams.

PART OF THE GROUND in the cornfield was thick with mud, making the wheels of the combine slide all over the place. Sara fought to bring the machine under control for what seemed the hundredth time. Her eyes were sore and gritty from lack of sleep, yet somehow she had to stay alert. It was Saturday again; the weekend was her only chance to push ahead with harvesting.

Sara circled around, ready to make another pass through the field. Now she was facing the dirt road that led to her farm. And coming along that road was the strangest procession. Sara brought herself to a rattling halt and peered out the grimy window of the cab. What in tarnation was going on?

Leading the procession were three huge combines rumbling, one after the other, picker heads spread out in front of them like monstrous claws. Following were a couple of grain trucks and then several cars and pickups. It didn't make any sense. What were all these people doing here with their machinery?

Sara scrambled down from her own combine and started jogging across the field. And that was when she saw Joshua Williams's sleek new Jeep pull up in front of her house. He swung out of the Jeep and Sara quickened her pace. She was thoroughly out of breath by the time she reached him.

"Dr. Williams—Joshua—what the heck is this all about?" The cold autumn air seemed to pinch her lungs, but she took in gulps of it as she waited for an answer.

Joshua was wearing a down vest in such a bright green color that it shimmered in the morning sun. Sara had to squint to look at it, rubbing her aching eyes. He leaned against the side of his Jeep.

"Good morning to you, too, Ms. Bennett. What you see here is your very own harvest crew, ready to start work. Namely, a group of my best students. I guarantee they'll be hard workers and get the job done for you."

College students were, indeed, spilling out from the combines, trucks and cars. They made a racket, laughing and talking with each other, their voices sharp and keen in the cold air. Sara rubbed her eyes again, as if she was only imagining all this and everyone would vanish as soon as she cleared her vision.

"Blast it, Joshua, I don't understand. You didn't bother to tell *me* about this. And I don't need any darn work crew to help me—"

"I didn't tell you because I knew that was exactly what you'd say. Don't worry, though. You don't have to feel beholden to anyone. My students are getting a lot out of this. It's a credit project for them, with quite a few extra points they can earn. It'll help them bump their grades up."

Sara felt anger burning her cheeks, a warmth in contrast to the crisp autumn air. She tugged impatiently at the zipper of her windbreaker. "You had no right to do this. No right at all! And I won't let you do it. Those machines can turn around and trundle the hell out of here again. I'll bring in my own harvest." She noticed that a couple of the students were glancing curiously in her direction. Taking hold of Joshua's bright green vest, Sara hauled him around to the back of the house where they could have a little more privacy.

"Okay, Dr. Williams," she began again. "This time you're going way too far. You come barreling in here, trying to take over. But you don't even believe in my dreams for the farm. You accuse my goats of being rowdy and you accuse *me* of harboring grandiose plans. And then you wonder why I don't want your help! Dammit, help like yours I don't need. I can handle my own life."

He rested his hands in the back pockets of his corduroy jeans. "Last week when I was out here it became very obvious to me that you *can't* handle everything in your life. But maybe nobody can, Sara. Maybe everybody needs help now and then."

"You're one to talk. You almost gave yourself pneumonia the night of that banquet—all because you refused to admit you couldn't give your speech yourself."

"That was different. A different case altogether." He seemed completely serious, standing there in the middle of her bedraggled garden with the usual obstinate expression on his face. Sara wanted to wail like one of her goats. But she knew she had to attack Joshua with logic. At least it was worth a try.

"Surely you can see how I feel. This is *my* farm. I know the lay of the fields, the tough spots. The way I'm juggling time and money these days, I can't afford a single mistake to be made."

"Just as I thought. You suffer from the delusion that you're the only one who can do justice to this farm. You act like the rest of us are treading uninvited on sacred ground."

"Listen, if you want to talk delusions, how about the one you have? The delusion that if you express the slightest emotion beyond sheer grouchiness, you'll compromise yourself—"

"Let's not get off the subject, Ms. Bennett. Here's the story. These kids are perfectly capable of harvesting your fields. Most of them grew up on farms. They'll be operating the same equipment they use to help their own parents at harvest time. Admit it, your argument isn't worth beans."

Sara leaned over and pulled a leaf from a shriveled iris. "Let's just say I want to do the work myself. Let's just say it's my choice, whether or not it makes any sense—whether or not it's practical or efficient or whatever. Whether or not you approve! Let's just say that I have the right to run my farm any darn way I see fit, without interference from the likes of you." Sara yanked another leaf, almost pulling the poor iris bulb from the ground. She was immediately contrite. "Sorry," she murmured to the iris. "I didn't mean to take out my frustrations on you."

"Lord, will you stop talking to plants? And be reasonable. You can't do this harvest on your own, plus keep up work and classes. You're a wreck, Sara. Your eyes are all red and you have circles under them. The other day you almost fell asleep in my horticulture seminar. I've been watching you all week, wondering when you were going to collapse."

His words held too much truth. Last night she'd really frightened herself when she'd dozed at the wheel of the combine and almost crashed through a fence. She didn't know how much further she could push herself with too much work and too little sleep.

"Those students have made an effort to come here this morning." She sighed wearily. "I suppose it would be uncivil of me to send them away after all their trouble. Not that I've agreed to this yet. I'm just considering all the angles."

"Fair enough." Joshua's face relaxed a little. He didn't go as far as smiling, but the look he gave Sara bordered on pleasant. A disturbing warmth suffused her, a warmth that no longer had anything to do with anger. In spite of his high-handed behavior, she was glad to be out talking to Joshua in her neglected garden. It no longer seemed quite so neglected with him in the middle of it. Why did she have to feel this surge of happiness, just at the sight of him?

"You're standing on some pink sundrops," she told him.

"What?" He gazed down at a haggard clump of grayish stems poking out of the dead grass.

"Used to be pink sundrops, anyway," Sara said mournfully. "They didn't do so well this year because I didn't give them the attention they needed. I hate making plants suffer. It's not fair." She patted her lopsided braid; she simply hadn't had time to do a proper job with it this morning. "Do I really look a wreck?"

"Pretty much."

Her garden was a shambles, so was her hair, and if she could believe Joshua, she had dark circles under her eyes. Sara had barely glanced in the mirror lately to find out what she looked like for herself.

"Okay, maybe I need a little help. But only a little! And it still makes me mad as anything that you interfered like this."

"Somebody had to." He began striding around to the front of the house, but Sara called to him.

"Wait. Joshua, just tell me one thing. Why did you really organize this work crew of yours? I mean, if I weren't so disgusted with you, I'd almost think you were being considerate. I'd almost think you cared a little about what happens to me." As soon as the words were out, she wished she hadn't said anything. She sounded as if she wanted him to care.

He hesitated, seemed about to answer, then stopped himself again. The lines of his face hardened. And when he did speak a moment later, his voice was cool.

"I saw that you had a problem, Ms. Bennett. Problems intrigue me and I like to solve them in the most effective way possible. That's all it is. You don't have to worry about being grateful."

"Believe me, I'm *not* grateful." Sara listened to herself and decided this conversation had become a ridiculous tangle. It would be better to end it as soon as possible. "I'm not grateful," she repeated, "but I'm going to say thank you, anyway. I know that doesn't make a whole lot of sense—but nothing between you and me seems to make any sense."

"You're welcome," he said dryly.

"Okay, then. Let's get everybody to work!"

A short while later Sara realized that her aggravation for the day had only begun. Joshua insisted on taking complete charge of the project, directing students as to where they should go and what work they should do. He started to look like a traffic cop, motioning away at the combines and grain trucks. Sara reflected dourly that she ought to supply him with orange gloves and a whistle. When she protested that by rights she should be the one to lead the crew, Joshua ordered her to go back to her own combine and leave him in peace to do his job.

The man was infuriating! He was practically taking over her farm. Sara would have been glad to argue with him about this at great length, but too many of the students seemed interested in her discussions with Joshua. And so she ended up back in the fields herself, plowing down cornstalks and having vitriolic arguments with Joshua in her imagination.

By late afternoon Sara had to admit that Joshua had chosen good students for his crew. One of the sophomores was able to repair a broken fan out at Sara's storage bins; fans were necessary to blow air up through the corn in the bins. Nothing was more important than keeping the moisture down in harvested corn and Sara was genuinely thankful. She found it a whole lot easier to express her gratitude to the students than to Joshua. Maybe it was because these college kids were so open and easy in their attitude. They were having fun today but it also made them feel good to be helping someone out. They were willing to admit that. Joshua, however, behaved as if this were nothing more than a well-orchestrated science project—with him doing all the orchestrating.

Toward the end of the day Sara had a brainstorm. She came up with an ideal way to show the students her appreciation for their hard work. Clambering into her old pickup, she made a run down the highway to the grocery store. When she returned, she instructed one of the students to tell the others what she planned for the evening. Apparently Sara's idea met with enthusiasm. By nightfall several young men and women were milling about in Sara's living room. Sara herself was in the kitchen, tearing open bags of corn chips and spooning avocado-and-onion dip into bowls. Joshua came striding into the kitchen, his down vest dusted all over with corn chaff. He frowned at Sara.

"This can't be right. People are telling me that you're giving a party."

"Well, that's exactly what I'm doing." She poured cranberry juice into Grandma Bennett's crystal punch bowl. "I think everyone deserves a party after today. The entire corn crop is in—what an accomplishment. All I have left is my soybean fields. This definitely calls for a celebration. I own a pretty good selection of records, as long as people don't mind listening to my dad's big-band albums. I think it's going to be fun."

"These kids don't need fun. I told you, they're getting extra credit for coming here and helping out. They don't need any other reward."

"I think they do," Sara said firmly. "And I'm in charge of *this* part of the day. You don't have to stick around, Joshua. You've already put in enough of your own time."

Joshua paced across the worn tile floor, leaving muddy boot prints behind him. Sara didn't mind the mud. But she was dismayed to find herself once again enjoying Joshua's presence. She hadn't seen him in a few hours and even in that short time she'd somehow started to miss him. She'd missed catching glimpses of his unruly thatch of red hair, his stubborn face, his body moving in a powerful and purposeful stride. But here he was now, striding purposefully back and forth in her kitchen.

"I'll have to stay," he said. "I'm responsible for this troop. They need a chaperon."

"They qualify as adults. They're eighteen, nineteen years old. Some are even twenty." Sara poured carbonated water in with the cranberry juice.

"Doesn't matter how old they are. They're my students. The work they did today was an official college project under my supervision. I can't stop supervising as long as they're on your farm.''

"So...stay," Sara told him in a casual voice, opening a package of chocolate-chip cookies. "I guess you don't have any choice." She admitted guiltily to herself that this was what she'd intended all along. Deep down, she'd planned this party with no one but cantankerous Dr. Joshua Williams in mind. No matter how ornery he was, she wanted one more excuse to be around him.

What on earth was she going to do with herself?

CHAPTER NINE

JOSHUA PICKED UP A chocolate-chip cookie and munched on it grumpily. "I hate parties," he said. "Especially parties with a bunch of my students, where I'm the oldest man in the room."

"You're so good with students in the classroom," Sara answered. "And you were good with them today, supervising. You were a bit dictatorial, I admit, but once I even heard you cracking a joke with a few freshmen. I should think you'd have a good time tonight." She arranged the rest of the chocolate-chip cookies on a plate. Joshua took another cookie.

"Parties are different," he said. "Damn useless occasions. Can't tolerate them."

"I like parties, myself."

"It figures. But I can't picture you hanging around with these students and having a good time. They're too young and callow for you."

Sara shuffled a stack of paper plates. "It's strange, you know. They're not that much younger than I am. Four, five, six years at the most. But you're right. I do feel so much older...maybe it's because I run my own farm, or because I left college for a while. Whatever the reason, sometimes I feel light-years older than the rest of them at school."

"You're more mature, that's what it is."

Sara glanced at him in surprise. "Dr. Williams, I don't believe it. I really don't."

He started in on another cookie. "What? Why are you looking at me like that?"

"You just paid me a compliment. A certifiable, bona fide compliment."

His expression turned sour. "Let's not get carried away, Ms. Bennett."

"You said I was mature. You can't get out of it—that's a compliment. I wish I had it recorded on tape." Sara happily stacked some paper cups. Joshua was a lot more human than he was willing to let on. Now and then, when his guard was down, he actually showed a more lenient side to his nature.

Sara shuffled another stack of paper plates. She knew she ought to take the refreshments to the students, but she wanted to linger with Joshua. This kitchen seemed just right with him here. She glanced around at all the familiar details: tarnished pots and pans hanging from hooks, layers of peeling wallpaper giving the walls a bumpy texture, Great-aunt Lucy's chair cushions turning threadbare, the rusty table lamp Sara had already rewired twice casting a soft glow over the room. Sometimes it seemed that everything Sara owned was rewired or repapered or repainted; she wondered if she possessed one item that was completely new. But it was Joshua's presence that brought a newness, a freshness into the place. He was vibrant and full of life, always carrying with him the green scent of growing things. Sara smiled, listening to the music that floated out to them from the living room. It was a Beatles song, lighthearted and whimsical, and she hummed along with it a little under her breath. Meanwhile, Joshua was surveying her with a critical eye.

"You look better than this morning," he pronounced. "But don't get excited. This isn't another compliment."

"I wonder what it is, then."

"An observation. I'm making an observation, that's all. In the same way I'd remark that these cookies are palatable." Joshua ate another chocolate-chip cookie, as if to prove his point. Sara stirred her punch, even though it didn't need stirring. She was glad she'd taken the time from harvesting to shower and wash her hair. Her hair was still damp, but it hung in a thick, shining ripple almost to her waist. She'd even hauled out the iron again, freshening up her black-and-red checkered shirtdress. Now the flannel cloth was soft against her skin and she felt quite womanly with Joshua's gaze upon her.

"You might as well take off your coat and act like you're going to stay a while," she suggested.

He seemed doubtful as to the advisability of this, but then shrugged out of his down vest and tossed it over a chair back. He was wearing another of his bright plaid shirts, this one in flannel. It appeared both she and Joshua favored flannel; they had that in common, at least.

One of the students burst into the kitchen. "Anything to eat?" he asked hopefully.

"Yes . . . yes, of course." Sara was sorry for the interruption, but she started gathering up cups, avocado dip and tortilla chips. Joshua took charge of the punch bowl, bearing it in front of him as if it were a weapon. The music blared in the living room, several couples dancing. Sara set her things down on the sideboard and headed back to the kitchen for the other refreshments. Joshua was right on her heels.

"I'll help," he said with determination. Sara couldn't avoid smiling again. Whether by choice or necessity, Joshua was aligning himself with her. Two groups had coalesced in the house: the students, and the small but complete group consisting of Joshua and Sara. She was pleased with that. Together she and Joshua carried the rest of the food into the living room. And together they took up a station next to the sideboard. Sara had pushed all the furniture against the walls so there'd be more room for dancing. She'd turned on only a few lamps, allowing for a shadowy, romantic atmosphere. Now someone discovered her father's big-band collection and several enthusiastic couples launched into the swing. This number was followed by a slow, seductive song. The couples started dancing close, clinging to each other.

Joshua was still working on the chocolate-chip cookies. He waved one in the air, gesturing at the couples. "Think we should let them do that?" he asked.

"Come on, Dr. Williams," Sara teased him. "Surely you've danced like that yourself on one or two occasions."

"Nope. Ever since my parents tried to turn me into a tap dancer, I can't tolerate any type of dancing."

Sara read it as a good sign, the casual way Joshua referred to his parents and to his short-lived career as a tap dancer. He was loosening up around her; she was sure of it.

"Well, no one should miss out on this kind of dancing. Slow and relaxing. Why don't you try it with me?"

"You've got to be kidding. Right here?"

"Right here, that's the idea. This is an excellent opportunity."

"Forget it, Ms. Bennett. We're the chaperons."

"No one here cares about that." Sara felt reckless, the way she had last weekend when she'd invited Joshua to stay for supper. She took hold of his hand and began tugging him toward the middle of the room. The only problem was that he refused to be tugged. He scowled at Sara in the dim light.

"No way, Ms. Bennett. I don't dance!"

"In my capacity as your assistant, I've determined that it would be perfectly harmless for us to share a dance. It might even be beneficial. It could promote goodwill between us, for once."

"Dammit, I won't joke about this."

"I'm not joking," she said with a surge of exasperation. "I believe in propriety just as much as you do. I simply don't see anything improper about two rational adults dancing to a 1940s record. Only I'm starting to wonder if one of us *is* rational."

His fingers tightened on hers, his touch sending a pleasurable yet oddly disturbing quiver of sensation through her. Joshua's expression turned grim. After a charged moment, he began to do some tugging of his own. He dragged Sara back to the kitchen, firmly shutting the living-room door behind him.

"All right, I see that I no longer have any choice," he said. "You're never going to understand my position unless I explain what happened with my other research assistant. So I'm going to explain."

The music drifting in from the living room changed again to a lively beat. But it was a muted sound, a backdrop. All of Sara's attention was focused on Joshua. She pulled a chair out and motioned to it.

"You'd better sit down and tell me everything," she said. "I think it's time."

He thumped down in the chair she'd indicated, its fussy, ruffled cushion only highlighting his masculinity. He reached across the table to shake out the last few crumbs from the chocolate-chip cookie bag. Sara rummaged through the grocery sacks and found another bag of cookies—coconut macaroons. She pushed them across to Joshua and sat down opposite him.

He ate three macaroons in a row. His voice was tense when he spoke. "It happened before I came to Glenn State. I was teaching at a private university in Minnesota. I was assigned a graduate student as my assistant, and according to her record she promised to be a competent worker. But letting her work for me turned out to be one of the biggest mistakes I've ever made."

Joshua seemed to require more macaroons before he went on. Sara waited patiently while he chewed, her hands clasped on the table in front of her. And he did go on.

"I never once intimated to my assistant that I had any personal interest in her. That was easy, because I *wasn't* interested in her. However, she started to make…inconvenient overtures. I told her to knock it off. She responded by showing up in my office one afternoon, dressed in nothing but her B.V.D.s.''

Listening to this, Sara began to feel the need for some macaroons, too. She pulled the cookie bag toward her and started munching. "You have an interesting way of putting things, Dr. Williams...B.V.D.s. But I get the picture."

Joshua's face had turned red. He looked beleaguered. "There I was. I had this cuckoo woman running around my office in her undies, proclaiming very loudly that she knew I wanted her. The dean was due in five minutes for a meeting with me and I didn't know how to get rid of the damn girl. Unfortunately, she took care of that part herself. When the dean knocked on my door, the demented woman climbed out my window to escape." Joshua groaned, as if he could see these past events all too clearly even now. Sara passed the macaroons back to him and tried to be reassuring.

"Well, it doesn't sound so bad, after all," she said. "You were spared explaining to the dean why you had this...uh, rather scantily clad assistant in your office. Thank goodness she had the sense to climb out the window."

"You don't understand, Ms. Bennett. The campus reporter was on the spot. It's my belief that my assistant arranged for him to be positioned strategically just outside. He snapped several good pictures of the half-naked woman climbing out my window."

"Oh, dear. That *is* unfortunate." Sara stopped eating mid-macaroon, but she had to fight a grin. The thought of reserved Joshua Williams with a half-naked woman climbing out his office window was entertaining. "Surely no one blamed you," she said. "I mean, you're so...upright and honorable. Surely everyone knew it was all your assistant's doing."

"I was exonerated, yes. But that didn't stop those photographs from appearing in the student newspaper. It didn't stop the ridiculous rumors from circulating. It didn't stop my next assistant from batting her eyes at me...or those embarrassing love poems from female students. I went on teaching at that university for a while longer, but then the opportunity at Glenn State came along and I took it. I promised myself that never, *never* again would I let the same thing happen to me."

Sara brushed coconut crumbs into a little pile on the table. "I'm glad you told me all this, Joshua. I wish you'd told me sooner. I understand how much you like your privacy and it must have been dreadful to have it ripped away like that. I sympathize."

"Dammit, I don't want your sympathy. I just want you to start being—different. Lord, I can't believe I'm having to contend with more rumors. I'm starting to think I'm cursed or something, when it comes to research assistants."

Sara stiffened at that. She spread both hands on the nicked surface of the table. "Hold on. I don't think you need to compare me to any of your other assistants. For one thing, I would never prance around somebody's office in my—my bloomers. And I never bat my eyes! I'm fairly honorable myself, Dr. Williams. When I fell asleep at your house, it was an unfortunate accident. I didn't plan it. And I sure as hell didn't have any photographers lurking outside."

"Okay, relax," Joshua said in a gruff voice. "I'm not accusing you of anything. I know it wasn't something you intended, that night at my house. The hectic way you run your life, I'm surprised you don't fall asleep more often in odd places. One of these times I expect to find you stretched out in the greenhouse or the conservatory, snoring away."

Sara supposed she'd been acquitted, although she resented any implication that she snored. "I'm very sorry about what happened to you. It was completely unfair. But I'll be honest. I think you've overreacted to the whole thing." She held up a hand to keep him from protesting, then noticed the cookie crumbs on her fingers. She brushed them off.

"Hear me out on this," she insisted. "The way I see it, you're an intensely private person, trying all your life to escape the histrionic atmosphere of your family. So when all of a sudden this gossip about you is splashed across the front pages of a newspaper, complete with photographs, and the other repercussions...well, of course you'd overreact. That's natural. You'd want even more privacy than before. And you'd be hypersensitive to the slightest hint that your privacy would be invaded again."

Joshua drew his eyebrows together. "Spare me any further analysis, Ms. Bennett."

"I like analyzing you. It's one of the few ways I can gain insight into your personality. Now and then you tell me something about your life, but then you clam up again. Like right now. You've started to clam up instead of continuing our discussion in a straightforward manner."

He ran both hands through his unruly hair. "This isn't supposed to be a discussion. How the hell did it turn into a discussion? All I wanted to tell you was...damn. My conversations with you never come out the way I intend!"

Sara leaned earnestly across the table toward him. "Joshua, if things keep getting all mixed up between us, it's because you're still trying to repress your feelings."

"Hey, not that. Not the 'R' word. Don't tell me about repression."

"Let me guess. You don't like that word because people in your family use it. They constantly tell you not to repress your emotions."

"Ms. Bennett, you do have some discernment, after all. Congratulations." Joshua chewed morosely on another macaroon.

"I have a lot of discernment. Look, maybe your family *is* too histrionic, too emotional. I'll grant that possibility. But you've gone too far the other way. You've overreacted to your family, just like you over-reacted about your assistant running around in her underwear." Sara grabbed another cookie herself. She felt compelled to burst out like this with Joshua, creating a sort of counterpoint to his reticence. The less he revealed, the more she pushed him to reveal. And this time, apparently, she'd pushed him too far. He stood up so abruptly that he almost sent his chair careening over backward.

"I've had enough trouble with research assistants. And you, Ms. Bennett, are causing even more trouble than the lady who hopped around my office half naked."

Sara stood up, too, and stalked over to confront
Joshua. "It really bugs the heck out of me that you'd
compare me to some girl who runs around people's
offices practically in the altogether. That just really
irritates me."

They glared at each other. Music pulsed from the
living room in a sensual beat. Joshua shifted position. So did Sara. It was as if she and Joshua had
started a wary sort of dance, after all. Sara's gaze
traveled to Joshua's mouth and then she forgot to be
angry at him. She longed for his kiss. And she longed
to have his arms around her.

Sara didn't know who made the first move, her or
Joshua. But suddenly, wonderfully, she *was* in his
arms. And at last Joshua was kissing her. Their kiss
was almost a frantic one, as if they had both gone too
long without water and had finally found something
to drink. Joshua buried his hands in her hair and
murmured her name against her lips. "Sara...Sara."
His voice was husky, with a tenderness that made her
yearn for more. She ran her fingers over the flannel
cloth of his shirt, and never had flannel seemed so
luxurious to her. Oh, the feel of it, soft from wear, soft
from molding itself to Joshua's strong muscles, warm
under her hands.

This kiss, this embrace offered so many sensations.
Sara didn't know how to capture them all. She'd
waited, it seemed, forever for this moment, and now
she was afraid she'd miss something important. Some
delightful detail would escape. She had to remember
everything: the pounding of Joshua's heart against her
own, the music drifting around them, the way Joshua's lips tasted subtly of coconut....

"Excuse me!" Joshua and Sara jumped apart, for all the world as if someone had fired a shotgun in the air. Sara turned toward the door, rather dazed. She saw one of the younger students, a freshman girl, staring at her and Joshua with widened eyes. The girl looked startled, then amused. "Um... I was just trying to find some more punch."

Sara took a bottle of cranberry juice from the counter and handed it over. Clutching the bottle, the girl edged away. "Thank you. Really. Don't mind me. Just go back to...whatever you were doing." The girl shut the door again with a satisfied bang.

Sara turned to Joshua again. He looked thunderous, all traces of tenderness vanished.

"Dammit, Ms. Bennett. Look what you did this time!"

"Seems to me we were both willing participants. I sure wish nobody had seen, but that kiss happened. And I'm glad it happened." Sara realized that every detail remained clear. Yes, Joshua's kiss was imprinted on her; its memory was intact.

She began to fear that the memory was all she'd ever have. Because Joshua's face had closed. Now he seemed more remote than he'd ever been. His eyes were as cold and hard as the water of a frozen gray lake.

"Ms. Bennett, that's it. That's finally it. This time... you're fired, for sure!"

SARA WIGGLED HER FEET impatiently, gazing at the scuffed toes of her buckaroo boots. She picked up a magazine, then set it down again. Joshua picked up his own magazine, flipping through it so fast that the pages sent a slight breeze in Sara's direction. Then he tossed it back on the table, too, and glared at Sara. She glared at him in return. The silent messages between them were potent. The messages had to be silent, because they were sitting outside the dean's office and the dean's secretary seemed inordinately interested in anything that transpired between Joshua and Sara.

At last the secretary plugged herself into a Dictaphone and began tapping away at a computer keyboard. Joshua took the opportunity to lean toward Sara.

"We wouldn't have been called to this damnable meeting if it hadn't been for you, Ms. Bennett."

"Wrong, Dr. Williams," Sara whispered fiercely. "*You're* the one who took a simple little kiss and blew it up into a major war."

"You started the war by kissing me in the first place, Ms. Bennett."

"I've thought it over, Dr. Williams. And I've come to realize that you're the one who initiated that kiss. Yes, you did. I was standing there in my kitchen, minding my own business and—"

"The trouble with you, Ms. Bennett, is that you never mind your own business."

"Well, neither do you, Dr. Williams. Neither do you!"

Sara became aware that the dean's secretary had stopped typing. The woman had even slipped off her earphones, cocking her head expectantly toward Joshua and Sara. Now Joshua glared at the secretary.

"I'm sure it won't be too much longer before the dean will be free," she said. "He's very anxious to meet with both of you."

"I'm sure," Joshua muttered.

"Oh, yes, he is. He canceled another appointment and rearranged a conference call just so he could...um, discuss matters between you and Ms. Bennett."

Joshua disappeared grouchily behind another magazine. The secretary waited a moment, obviously hoping that Joshua and Sara would start arguing again. Then, with an air of disappointment, the woman went back to her Dictaphone.

Sara drummed her heels against the floor, wondering if the whole campus knew by now that she and Joshua had kissed in the kitchen of her farmhouse. Some weeks had passed since the incident. In that time Sara had managed to harvest her soybean crop, had finished writing two seminar papers and had compiled a data base program for Joshua's lesson plans. She'd even been getting a little more sleep. In spite of all this productivity, however, her life had been impossible. Dr. Joshua Williams was making it impossible!

He wouldn't forgive that one kiss. He behaved as if it had totally disrupted his life. And meanwhile Sara couldn't forget the dratted kiss, either. She'd start daydreaming about it at the most importune times. Like right now, for instance. Right now she was thinking about the way Joshua had tangled his hands in her hair, the way he had murmured her name with such desire. She was thinking about the way his lips had captured hers....

As if he could sense her thoughts, Joshua lowered his magazine and scowled at her. She dived behind her own magazine, trying unsuccessfully to concentrate on an article about the trend toward nontraditional student enrollment on college campuses. With her twenty-fifth birthday looming near, Sara qualified as a nontraditional student, but that wasn't the half of it. At the moment she was engaged in a nontraditional battle with a very nontraditional and obnoxious professor. A professor who sure as heck knew how to kiss...

A buzzer sounded on the secretary's telephone. She left her desk and floated toward the dean's office, giving Joshua a conspiratorial wink as she went by. He rattled his magazine, grumbling under his breath. As soon as the secretary had disappeared into the office and closed the door behind her, Joshua leaned toward Sara again.

"It's still not too late to stop this nonsense, Ms. Bennett. All you have to do is go in there to the dean and announce that you're requesting a transfer."

"And all you have to do is go in there and apologize for the ruckus you've been making."

"You've been making your own ruckus, Ms. Bennett."

"Purely as a defense mechanism. You know, Dr. Williams, if you'd simply ignored that kiss, everyone would have forgotten about it by now."

"How the devil would you expect me to ignore a kiss like that?" His eyes narrowed as his gaze lingered on her mouth. She flushed.

"All right, so it wasn't exactly an ignorable kiss. It was more...a memorable kiss. But that doesn't mean we have to let it turn us into enemies."

"I don't want to be enemies with you, Ms. Bennett. I just want you...out of my life."

Sara was stung, but darned if she'd show it. "I *will* be out of your life—when I graduate. Why can't you tolerate my presence quietly until then? It's not for very long. Just a matter of weeks, really."

Joshua rattled his magazine once more. "We're talking principles here. Principles have to be defended."

"If you want to know my opinion, the only thing you're defending is your own pigheadedness."

"I don't want your opinion, Ms. Bennett."

"I'll give it to you anyway. Here's the real problem. You refuse to admit that you were responsible for that kiss in my kitchen. It was *your* kiss and you won't even acknowledge it. Basically, you've disowned a kiss that you yourself engendered."

"Lord, you make it sound like I disinherited a child."

"All I'm saying is that you ought to claim your own kisses, when they rightfully belong to you. Think about it, Dr. Williams. If you hadn't come out to my farm that day with your work crew, nothing would have happened."

"I was only trying to help you," he said gruffly. "Are you still blaming me for that, too?"

Sara shifted in her chair. "No...yes...I don't know! I can't figure you out, dammit. Part of me says that you're as kindhearted as mush, under that infuriating exterior of yours. The other part tells me that you've become so clinical and scientific, there's no hope left for you at all."

"Don't start hoping anything about me, Ms. Bennett. Whatever happened in your kitchen that night—it won't happen again."

Sara wanted to hit him over the head with a whole stack of magazines. "I'm not hoping, believe me. Who the heck said I was hoping?"

The dean's secretary came sailing back out of his office. "Dean Logan will see you now," she proclaimed. She lowered her voice to add, "I warn you, he's not in a good mood. He's never in a good mood lately when he thinks about the two of you."

Sara and Joshua stood up at the same time. They looked at each other. Joshua's expression was implacable. It was obvious that he wasn't going to back down. But Sara wasn't going to back down, either. It was no longer simply a matter of needing the money from her job. This war with Joshua had become a matter of principle for *her*, too. She lifted her chin.

"I'm ready," she said. "I don't care what kind of mood anybody's in . . . I'm ready."

And then, together, she and Joshua went into the dean's office.

CHAPTER TEN

DR. HOWARD LOGAN, the Dean of Plant Sciences, was a tall, untidy man. His thinning hair stood in clumps, as if he'd been pulling on it. His tie was knotted haphazardly and he had an ink stain on his cheek. In spite of this personal disorder, his office was neat and controlled—papers lined up precisely on the desk, books alphabetized on the shelves, computer screen buffed to a polish. Dean Logan gave both Joshua and Sara an impassive perusal as they sat down opposite him.

"Good afternoon, Josh...Ms. Bennett."

"Good afternoon," Sara answered politely. Joshua, however, dispensed with any formalities.

"Howard," he said. "Let's get right to the point. Sara—Ms. Bennett, that is, needs a transfer. I need a new research assistant. What's the holdup?"

Dr. Logan's calm expression didn't change, but a slight crease had appeared in his forehead. Sara wondered if the crease constituted a frown.

"Josh, I'm afraid you and Ms. Bennett have created the holdup all on your own. Let's examine how matters stand." Dean Logan reached for a wire basket on the corner of his desk. He angled the basket in front of him. "Form B-29," he intoned. "Personnel Action Notice to transfer Ms. Bennett, filed by Dr. Williams. Form 43-D, Employee Deposition, filed by you, Ms. Bennett, against Dr. Williams." The dean dug deeper into the basket. "Form 1196-P, Motion to Dismiss Employee Grievance, filed by Dr. Williams against Ms. Bennett. Form S-94, Motion to Counter Dismissal, filed by Ms. Bennett. Form 300-W, Faculty Objection Sheet, filed by Dr. Williams against Ms. Bennett—etcetera, etcetera, ad infinitum!"

Dean Logan's scrupulous portrayal of calm disintegrated. He threw several of the aforementioned forms up into the air. They landed helter-skelter on his desk again; one six-part form skidded along the floor. It was like an explosion suddenly taking place over a quiet landscape. Sara watched Dean Logan with alarm, wondering how big this explosion would get. It was easy to picture the dean's secretary trying to keep him all neat and tidy...and then him disrupting things by pulling on his hair or throwing papers to the sky.

The dean's outburst was brief. He sat back in his chair and folded his arms. His expression smoothed out except for that one telltale crease across his brow.

"Now, Ms. Bennett. Josh. Apparently you have become overly fond of the bureaucratic maze at our college. In the last month alone you've filed I don't know how many motions and grievances and dismissals against each other. Not to mention all the countermotions, countergrievances and counterdismissals. Between the two of you, you've supplied sufficient paperwork to keep me buried up to my neck for the rest of my natural-born life."

Sara decided this was an attempt at humor on the dean's part. She gave him an encouraging smile. He didn't smile back. Instead he swiveled slightly in his chair, as if another explosion was imminent.

"It seems to me that perhaps we can come to a different arrangement," he said. "Perhaps it's not too much to hope that both of you can resolve your differences in a more . . . clear-cut fashion."

Joshua rubbed his jaw. "Howard, I don't like college bureaucracy any more than you do. But I don't see any other solution."

"Have you attempted to discuss the problem, whatever it is, with Ms. Bennett?"

"Ms. Bennett refuses to see reason—"

"I'm afraid I've already discussed matters with Dr. Williams several times," Sara interrupted. "It's done no good."

The dean began to swivel a little more vigorously in his chair. Sara kept a wary eye on him as he spoke.

"Josh, Ms. Bennett. I don't like being an arbitrator, but you leave me no choice. Several confusing stories have been circulating around campus about the two of you. Perhaps if you would clarify those stories for me, we could come to terms. Because that's what I'd like. That's my goal. I would like you both to come to terms, here in my office, before this goes any further. Josh, perhaps you could tell me exactly what your complaint is in regard to Ms. Bennett."

Joshua cleared his throat. "It's all right there on the forms. Incompatibility."

The crease in Dean Logan's forehead deepened. "Perhaps you could be more specific. You could give me individual examples of your complaints against Ms. Bennett. May I say that I find nothing specific on any one of these forms." His hands hovered near the papers, as if he was about to toss them up in the air again.

Joshua glanced over at Sara, frowning. He paused for a moment and then gave a curt shrug. "I can't offer you any specific examples."

"None?"

"None."

Sara crossed her legs and smoothed her denim skirt. This was just like Joshua. He could be perverse, annoying, aggravating for days on end—and then, out of the blue, he'd do something to reaffirm how upright he was. How honorable. All during his battle with Sara, he'd never once said or done anything in public to denigrate her reputation. And he was refusing to do so now.

The dean kept on swiveling in his chair in suppressed agitation. "Would you say therefore that Ms. Bennett is a good worker?" he asked.

"Yes, I suppose I would say that."

"Well, finally," Sara exclaimed. "It's about time you said it."

Joshua looked so disgusted, you'd think he'd just swallowed a root ball. Meanwhile, the dean swiveled in Sara's direction.

"Ms. Bennett, perhaps *you* can shed some light on this unfortunate situation. What are your complaints against Dr. Williams? Please . . . be specific."

Sara smoothed out her skirt some more. "I'm sorry, but I've already tried to be as specific as possible. Dr. Williams and I are uncongenial, just as I've stated on Form 43-D."

"That's it?"

"That's it."

Dean Logan's cheeks puffed out with air, as if pressure was growing inside him and any minute he truly *would* explode. Sara began to wonder if the dean's life was a constant struggle between chaos and order. She suspected he wanted order more than anything, but chaos continually threatened him...especially when he was confronted with a predicament like that of Joshua and Sara.

Making a decided effort, Dean Logan finally blew the air out of his cheeks. "Very well. I see that this tactic won't bring us any success. Let's try a new one. I believe that the two of you need to get on neutral ground for a little while in order to discuss your differences. And I know just how to accomplish that. The Mile High Elementary School in Denver has requested that we supply judges for its annual science fair. You, Josh—and you, Ms. Bennett, will be those judges. Next week you will travel to Denver together."

"Together?" Sara and Joshua echoed in dismay.

"That's right. Together. You will spend the day in a cooperative endeavor. Most important, you will spend the day resolving your problems."

Joshua shook his head. "Howard, this doesn't make any sense. Ms. Bennett and I—we could fly off to Tahiti and it still wouldn't solve our problems. What good will a day in Denver do us? I'm afraid I can't agree to this."

"I'm afraid I can't either," Sara added. "When it comes to Dr. Williams and me...I just don't think we'll find neutral territory anywhere."

"Ms. Bennett and I have already attempted cooperative endeavors," Joshua said grimly. "And I think we'd both agree they didn't work out."

"I can recall a *few* moments of cooperation," Sara retorted. She was thinking about that kiss in her kitchen, and she knew Joshua caught her meaning. Once again his gaze lingered on her mouth.

"Some types of cooperation are best left alone," he said in a distracted voice.

"I'd be willing to leave them alone if you would."

"I'm willing, dammit." He continued to gaze at her intently. Sara felt an unsettling quiver of sensation go through her, just to have Joshua looking at her like that.

"I'm glad you realize that noncooperation is the only solution for us," she said stiffly.

"You're the one who needs to realize it, Ms. Bennett. You need to realize once and for all that we'll have no further cooperation."

"Believe me, I look forward to a *complete* lack of cooperation, Dr. Williams—"

Dean Logan slapped both hands down on his desk, sending more forms skittering to the floor. Now surely he was going to lose control. But his voice was quite calm when he began speaking.

"Enough. The two of you will learn to cooperate, if it's the last thing you do. You'll both be going to Denver next week. Together. You'll judge the science fair. If you don't agree to my terms, I'll file Form 765-Q, Motion to Restrain Contrary Botanists and Fractious Research Assistants. In other words, I want both of you out of my hair. And please understand this—once you leave for Denver, neither one of you will return to Glenn State until you've resolved your problems. All of them.

"Now, good day, Ms. Bennett. Good day, Josh. I need some peace!"

SARA STOOD ON HER front porch, shivering in the frosty morning air. She cursed her own vanity. Today Joshua was picking her up for the drive into Denver, and she'd been overwhelmed by a perverse need to look pretty for him. Her frayed parka simply hadn't seemed acceptable. She'd opted instead for a light gabardine jacket that looked quite stylish with her checkered flannel shirtdress. And now she was freezing, all for the sake of impressing a man who refused to be impressed with her.

His shiny blue Jeep came up the drive and stopped in front of her house. Sara hurried down the porch steps and climbed in, her teeth fairly rattling with cold. Joshua glanced over at her and immediately turned up the heat.

"Thank you," she said through her chattering teeth.

"You should have waited for me inside. And, Lord, don't you have anything warm to wear?"

"This is warm."

"Right, and I'm the King of Siam." Joshua shrugged out of his down vest and without ceremony wrapped it around her shoulders. This was even better than the blast of the heater. Now Joshua's warmth enveloped her, intimate warmth that had been captured in his bright green vest. Sara struggled to remind herself that she was only taking this trip with him under duress. The dean had insisted on it—so here she and Joshua were, forced to spend the day together. Somehow they had to resolve their differences, but Sara wasn't very hopeful on this point. During the past week, the tension between herself and Joshua had escalated. At the college they spoke to each other only when absolutely necessary, working in a strained silence. Always there was the sense that a storm might break at any moment. But it didn't break; the tension simply grew and they became even more rigidly polite with each other as the days passed.

Now Sara buckled her seat belt while Joshua turned the Jeep around and headed for the highway. She tried to think of something noncombative to say.

"Nice vehicle," she managed at last.

"It's too new. I don't like new cars. But my old four-wheel drive finally gave out and I had to get a replacement."

"Seems like you made a good choice."

"Hmmph."

Well, so much for a discussion of Joshua's transportation history. They were on the highway now, the Jeep accelerating. Sara tried another topic.

"How's Laddie?" she asked.

"Fine. His arthritis is acting up a little, but I think he'll be okay."

"I hope so. How long have you had him?"

Joshua hesitated, and Sara realized he considered this subject too personal for sharing. Goodness, the man was prickly about guarding his privacy. Sara decided to forget about being noncombative.

"It's obvious you've had Laddie a very long time. And it's obvious you care about him a great deal, even though you don't want to show it when I'm there."

"Okay, okay. It was years ago, when I was still in college. One of my sisters was dating some guy who bred collies and she ended up with Laddie. Then she broke up with the guy and couldn't stand having a collie around any more. Said it reminded her too much of her ex-boyfriend. So I took the darn dog. End of story."

"You really *are* a soft touch, aren't you, Dr. Williams?"

"You're psychoanalyzing me again, Ms. Bennett. Why I do things is none of your business."

Sara examined this glimpse Joshua had given her into his life. It confirmed what she'd already suspected about him: he was, indeed, a soft touch. And once he took on something as his responsibility, he would never abandon it. Flights of emotion would never get in the way of his quiet dedication to Laddie.

Sara gazed at his strong capable hands, gripping the steering wheel. Oh, damn. She was thinking admiring thoughts about him. And that was dangerous. Joshua was so clearly a man who didn't admire *her*. She couldn't afford to care too deeply about what he thought. After graduation she'd probably never see him again. That was what he wanted, anyway. It had to be what she wanted, too.

She stared out the windshield of the Jeep. Brown fields spread along either side of the road, only a stubble of corn left in the frozen ground. Farmers just like Sara had harvested these fields. Other people shared her dreams; she didn't need Joshua to share them. This thought gave her fortitude. It made her believe she could have a reasonable discussion with Joshua while keeping her emotions at bay.

"You know," she said, "the dean was right about one thing. We have to resolve our problems before they get out of hand."

"I see only one resolution. You resign your position with me. Transfer voluntarily."

"No. I won't do that. The solution is for you to retract Form B-29."

"I like Form B-29. I'm starting to develop a real fondness for Form B-29. I want Form B-29 in my life."

Sara found her capacity for reasonableness severely tested. "Why can't you just admit what's really bothering you about us?" she burst out. "Why can't you do that for once?"

"First of all, there isn't any 'us.' There's you, there's me. No 'us.'" Joshua didn't look at her when he spoke; he wasn't one of those drivers who had to be in constant eye contact with his passengers until you thought for sure he was going to crash. Sara liked the fact that Joshua's gaze remained steady on the road. And it annoyed the heck out of her that she could find something else to admire about him, right in the midst of an argument.

"That's where you're mistaken, Dr. Williams. Somehow, even though neither one of us wanted it, an 'us' has developed. We can control it, we can beat it down—but only if we acknowledge its existence."

"You make it sound like we're in a horror movie and any minute now we'll be attacked by the 'us' monster."

"I've seen enough horror movies to know that you have to be prepared if you're going to defeat the monster. You have to recognize exactly what the monster is, you have to study it from all angles—"

Joshua groaned. "I'm sorry I ever made the analogy. Okay, Ms. Bennett, somehow we've created this 'us.' What do you suggest to vanquish it?"

She wondered if that was humor she heard in his voice. She could never tell for sure with Joshua. Most of the time he was serious or gruff, but his sense of irony would break through at odd moments, always in a quiet, subtle way.

"The first thing we do is admit exactly how we feel about each other. I'll start. Basically... it really exasperates me that my life is being disrupted by another man who can't express his emotions. You'd think I would've gotten over that after the experience with Ben Timmond. You'd think I would learn."

"Tell me more about this Ben Timmond."

Sara knew Joshua was deliberately steering the conversation in a new direction, but for some reason she wanted to talk about Ben. And she wanted to talk about him to Joshua, of all people. She couldn't explain it.

"Ben's parents have a farm not too far from mine. We knew each other in high school, but it wasn't until we got to college that we started dating. At first I thought we were just right for each other. I thought Ben was a steady sort of person, someone I could count on. And we both wanted to farm, there was never any question about that. It was just that... everything between us was so darn placid. So lacking in passion. Ben could never say he loved me, or that he couldn't live without me, or that he thought about me all the time. He did say that he liked me and he enjoyed my company and he hoped we'd have a satisfying long-term relationship together."

"And that's why you broke up with him?" Joshua asked dryly.

"That's exactly why. The day it happened was rather awful. I'd finally told Ben that I loved him, but he just couldn't say the words back to me. And that was when I knew we'd never have more than a very solid and placid future together and the whole thing would make me absolutely miserable."

Joshua still kept his eyes on the road, but he shook his head. "Expressing emotions doesn't count for a whole lot. You've just given the perfect example. You told this Timmond guy that you loved him, but apparently you didn't really mean the words."

"Of course I meant them," Sara said indignantly. "I hurt for quite a while after Ben and I broke up. He allowed the breaking up to happen so easily, that was what hurt the most. It was fine with him if I stayed, fine if I left."

"That's only your own perspective. The guy probably hurt as badly as you did, but he just didn't know how to show it."

Sara considered this. "No..." she said thoughtfully. "I got to know Ben well enough, and I can say it was more than just not being able to express his feelings. He honestly was a tranquil person. He didn't get worked up about much of anything, including me. He wanted me for a partner, but he knew he could find another partner if I didn't work out. In fact, he got married six months after we broke up." Sara turned a little in her seat and studied Joshua.

"Now, you're different than Ben," she said. "I didn't realize how different until right this minute, talking about it. I've been trying to think you're the same as he is, but you're not. You're not tranquil at all. You have a mass of emotions seething inside you and just waiting to spring out at the world."

"Ms. Bennett, you continually use images that make me think I'm trapped in a horror movie."

"Don't try to change the subject again. The point is, you have all these emotions but you refuse to express them. But today is when you finally have to let them out. You have to admit you have *some* feelings about me so we can go back to the dean with a resolution."

"Sure. I'm supposed to go to the dean and say, 'Howard, I'm very attracted to Sara Bennett, but she drives me nuts because she's always expecting me to emote.'"

"You'd say that?" Sara asked with interest. "You'd say you were not only attracted to me, but very attracted—"

"Ms. Bennett, that's another thing about you that drives me nuts. I say anything, and you have to poke and prod at it to find out if there really is an emotion underneath."

"I have this theory that if I poke around long enough, I *will* find your emotions."

"Sara, forget about finding them. And here's some free advice. Stop putting so much importance on whether or not some guy's willing to spout off about romance. All my life I've lived with people who spout off about it. Practically every day of my childhood my parents had a big fight and afterward they'd swear that they'd never fight again. They'd have this big scene where they'd hug and make wonderful speeches about each other. It was a real production, with us kids as the audience. But the next day they'd be yelling at each other all over again. Then you have my sisters, always announcing that *this* time they've found true love. What happens? One of them falls in love with a dog breeder, but a week later she can't even stand the sight of a collie pup.''

"I understand," Sara said. "You think I'm like the people in your family. You think I want everything messy and emotional, but I don't know anything about constancy."

"I think you want everything messy and emotional, but you do know about constancy. You know too much about it. That's why you're hanging on to your farm against all rationality. You feel you have to be loyal to your parents' memory no matter what happens.''

"Dammit, Joshua, are you praising me or condemning me?''

"Neither. I'm stating a fact."

Sara was tempted to reach out and honk the Jeep's horn, loudly and belligerently. "You're condemning me, all right. I can just imagine what sort of woman you'd rather be with. A female clone of Ben Timmond. Someone all peaceful and quiet who never cares too deeply about anything and who never disturbs you by trying to poke around and find out what you're feeling."

"That does sound peaceful, if nothing else," Joshua remarked. Now Sara almost did reach over to thump the horn. He'd worked himself into a convenient position where he offered neither positive or negative comments. He was going too far with the dean's suggestion that Sara and Joshua find "neutral

ground.'' That wouldn't solve any problems at all. But
Sara lapsed into a dissatisfied silence, staring out the
windshield again.

The Jeep drove through a small town. The down-
town area was dusty and deserted, some of the shops
boarded up. Joshua was like one of those buildings,
with boards nailed over the windows to keep intrud-
ers out. Except that Joshua wasn't empty inside. He
was full of life and vibrancy that he didn't want anyone else to see. It was a shame. If Joshua Williams
truly *were* a building, Sara would tear down all the
boards and allow the sunlight to shine right through
the windows.

The image pleased her for a moment. Then she
glanced at Joshua and saw the hard outline of his
profile. He didn't want her to get too close to him; he
made that obvious in everything he did. She wasn't the
kind of woman he wanted. No . . . she wasn't Joshua's
kind of woman at all. He'd made that clear, too.

The thought depressed her inordinately. She leaned
back in her seat and closed her eyes, determined to get
some use out of this trip. Maybe she could rest a little; she still wasn't getting as much sleep as she needed.
But she couldn't relax here next to Joshua. Even with
her eyes closed, she was too aware of him. Sighing, she
straightened up again.

After another hour or so of strained silence, they
reached the outskirts of Denver. The pace of the traffic revved up, frenetic as always in this big city. But
Joshua refused to pick up his own pace. He drove
right at the speed limit, seemingly unperturbed by the
cars whizzing around him.

"You really must be the most stubborn man alive," Sara told him. "You won't fall in with the rest of the traffic. And it's sheer obstinacy on your part."

"Why should another car dictate how fast I drive?"

"And why should your research assistant dictate your emotions," Sara muttered.

"You've got the idea, Ms. Bennett."

Perhaps Joshua drove at his own pace, but he knew the city well. Making decisive yet well-thought-out lane changes—always using his turn signal—he exited the freeway and drove through a quiet residential section. The bare branches of trees made a stark tracery against the ice blue sky; lawns were clipped but had turned grayish green with the beginnings of winter. Eventually Joshua pulled into the parking lot of the Mile High Elementary School.

Sara unfastened her seat belt. "Well, we're here at last. Let's get on with this. Let's cooperate a little, as the dean would say."

But Joshua didn't unfasten his own seat belt. He drummed his fingers against the steering wheel, looking extremely disgruntled.

"What's wrong?" Sara asked. "We have to do this—brought it on ourselves, I suppose."

"Dammit, I'm no good with kids," Joshua grumbled. "With college students, it's different. I can talk to them. But eight- and nine-year-olds...I don't know what to do with them. They're too short, for one thing. And they always seem to have sticky fingers."

Sara looked him over. "You do have a tendency to disappear when we get groups of kids in the conservatory."

"You're good at handling those tours. I don't mind leaving them to you."

"Careful, or you might give me another compliment."

"Lord, I don't know why I'm telling you any of this. We'll just go in there and get this science fair out of the way."

"It might actually be fun."

"Hah." Joshua swung out of his side and came around to open Sara's door. He had a habit of performing courteous gestures like this, even when grumbling about something or other.

Sara slid down from the Jeep and gazed at him. Joshua Williams, with his bright russet hair, his mismatched socks, his unexpected gallantry, his incredible stubbornness . . . why did she have to fall in love with this man? Why?

She was appalled at her own thoughts. Because it couldn't be true. She was attracted to the aggravating man, yes. But she wasn't falling in love with him. Surely she wasn't falling in love!

CHAPTER ELEVEN

THE MOUSETRAP WAS an intricate contrivance of gears, levers and pulleys. Altogether it was an impressive piece of machinery, and it actually worked. The ten-year-old boy who had invented it produced a fluffy white mouse. The mouse skittered through the metal passageway of the trap, pounced on a tidbit of cheese and began nibbling it. A small door like a castle gate rattled down into place, cutting off the mouse's escape route. Apparently this particular mouse had been through the routine before and didn't seem overly perturbed. It finished the cheese and then began scurrying around its prison. The prison, however, was more like a first-class hotel suite, equipped with all sorts of comforts for the mouse—a treadmill, a cozy nest of wood shavings, a complicated toy fashioned from bits of electrical wiring. The young inventor explained his rationale to Joshua and Sara.

"Mice get bored if they don't chew," said the solemn, dark-haired boy. "They like to chew on wood and electrical wiring. My idea is to keep the mouse happy and occupied after you catch him. And when he's had enough fun, you take him out to a field and you let him go."

"Hmm." Joshua rubbed his jaw. "Very interesting. You've created a combination mousetrap/entertainment center."

"That's right. That's my idea, exactly." The boy gave a pleased little smile, then quickly became solemn again.

Sara watched this exchange. Joshua didn't think he was good with kids, but so far today he'd been a hit with them. His secret seemed to be that he didn't condescend. He treated them with a respectful reserve, as if they were students in one of his biology classes at the college. Sara was impressed by the way he was handling this science fair and that put her in more of a turmoil than ever.

From the moment she and Joshua had walked into the gym of the Mile High Elementary School half an hour ago, her thoughts had been in confusion. Did she love Joshua? Surely not! She *couldn't* love him. He scoffed at her dreams for the farm, he wanted a placid woman completely unlike Sara, he refused to share his feelings . . . it would be a disaster all around to love a man like Joshua Williams.

"Ms. Bennett, are you ready to move on to the next exhibit?" he asked.

"Not just yet." Sara made one last perusal of the mousetrap, trying to concentrate on the science fair instead of on Joshua. She needed to be an impartial judge in spite of the swirl of her emotions. She jotted down a few notes on her pad, then followed Joshua to the next invention—the Super Duper Wallpaper Hanger.

The device was an all-in-one tool, bristling with attachments: wallpaper brush, pencil, trimming knife,

ruler, scissors, sponge. The inventor, a nine-year-old
girl with bangs flopping into her eyes, demonstrated
the tool with devastating skill. A mere flick of her
wrist sent a plumb line shooting down from the tool
like a yo-yo. With another flick, out shot a measuring
tape. Deftly the girl made some measurements on a
Sheetrock panel. After briefly soaking a roll of wallpaper in water, she slapped it up on the panel. Then,
with yet another flick of her wrist, the girl smoothed
out the wallpaper and sponged away excess glue. The
panel was exquisitely papered.

"Want to try it?" The inventor thrust her Super
Duper Hanger toward Sara and Joshua.

"Dr. Williams, you go ahead," Sara urged. Joshua
frowned at her. But he took the wallpaper tool in hand
and flicked his wrist masterfully. Unfortunately, his
flick was too masterful. The weight at the end of the
plumb line shot out so fast it almost bonged him on
the head. But Joshua proved he wasn't one to give up
easily. He worked on perfecting his wrist motion and
after several moments he'd papered his own panel.

"Not bad," said the inventor. "You need more
practice, though."

"Look, if I ever need any wallpapering done, I'll
just hire you," Joshua answered. "I'll pay the going
rate."

The nine-year-old inventor beamed and Sara knew
Joshua had won himself another "short" friend. He
probably still thought he wasn't any good with kids,
but he took them seriously and they loved that.

Love... blast it, why did that one word keep pop-
ping up whenever she thought about Joshua now? It
was very inconvenient. She didn't like this at all.

"Ms. Bennett, are you feeling okay?" Joshua asked in a gruff voice. "You look a little—I don't know, distraught, I suppose."

"No way am I distraught. Disgusted maybe, but not distraught."

"Hey, just checking." He strolled along to the next exhibit and Sara stalked after him. He actually seemed to be enjoying himself, in spite of his initial misgivings about the science fair. Sara was irked that she couldn't enjoy the day herself. She couldn't possibly enjoy it; she was tormented by the fear that it would be much too easy for her to love Joshua Williams, no matter what her better judgment told her.

Somehow she made her way through the rest of the science fair. The gym reverberated with enthusiastic noise. Kids and teachers and parents were all here, milling about in excitement. Sara did her very best to concentrate on each new invention, jotting down notes about a cat collar that glowed in the dark, a press for drying flowers, a reversible lamp shade and a musical fish tank. But always she was aware of Joshua beside her, his face serious, his concentration thorough as he examined each project for himself.

At last Sara and Joshua were ushered into one of the classrooms, where they were left alone for the important task of consulting about prizes to be awarded. Sara squeezed herself into a small chair. She gazed at a poster of a plump bear hibernating under a patchwork quilt.

"I hate having to choose winners," she said. "If it were up to me, every single one of those kids out there would be awarded a prize, just for having the ingenuity to come up with an invention."

"This is no time to be craven, Ms. Bennett. You have to be ruthless. They're allowed first prize, second prize, third prize. That's it." Joshua sat down in the teacher's chair. He looked imposing, even though a mobile of dangling plastic spiders hung right above his head. "Now, let's consider the possibilities. I was really impressed by that automatic dishwasher made out of squirt guns. But I also liked the mousetrap. Not to mention the fish tank that played 'My Bonnie Lies over the Ocean.' And the cookie-making machine. That was good, even though the cookies came out a little lumpy..."

"Joshua, you're just as softhearted as I am. You want to give everyone a prize, too."

"Okay, so maybe I do," he grumbled. "What about it?"

Sara struggled up from her small chair and came to stand on the other side of the desk. "Joshua..."

"Yes, Ms. Bennett?" He drew his eyebrows together, as if he wasn't looking forward to what she had to say. But there were some things that just had to be said. She realized that getting her turmoil out into the open was the only way to subdue it.

"Joshua, I've decided I'd better make one point very clear. Basically... I want you to know I wouldn't fall in love with you if you were the last botanist alive on this whole green earth."

A pained expression came over his face. "Who the devil said anything about love?"

"I did, just now. I'll confess I had a few bad moments today, thinking I *could* fall in love with you. It was a sort of aberration that came over me. But I've been fighting it and I feel better already. Because I need someone who'll express his feelings, someone who'll encourage my dreams instead of criticizing me. And that someone definitely isn't you!'' Sara paused. She did feel better—immensely relieved, in fact. She'd been right to get everything out in the open. But apparently her declaration of nonlove hadn't had a salutary effect on Joshua. He pushed back his chair and stood. The mobile of plastic spiders brushed his head and he swatted it impatiently.

''Hold on a minute. You act like there's actually a chance for something between us—''

''Well, maybe there is. Why don't you just admit it? It's the only sensible way to deal with this situation. We both have to admit the potential's there for us to do something idiotic like fall in love with each other.''

His frown deepened. ''Maybe you could be that idiotic, Ms. Bennett, but not me. No way.''

''I suppose you see any tendency to fall in love as a weakness you won't tolerate in yourself. I suppose you think it's something you can control by sheer force of will—just like the night of the banquet, when you tried to overpower your cold.''

''Ms. Bennett, you're poking and prodding again.''

''I wonder... will you ever let yourself fall in love with *anyone?* I mean, I'll be perfectly willing to fall in love with the right man if he ever comes along. But you—maybe you've sworn off the idea of love altogether.''

Joshua didn't answer. He just stood there beside the spider mobile, looking profoundly disgruntled. Sara had to do all her speculating about him on her own. And she was disturbed by what she ended up speculating. She had a hunch that if Joshua ever did express his emotions . . . if he ever did tell a woman that he loved her, he would mean the words with all his heart. He probably wouldn't say them very often, but he would mean them. And he would stick faithfully with one woman, just the way he'd stuck with his collie all these years. Sara felt an odd pain twist through her. It took her a moment to realize she was experiencing envy . . . envy for the woman Joshua might someday love with quiet, yet intense devotion.

Sara paced restlessly. What was wrong with her? She'd started mooning about Joshua all over again. She couldn't afford to do that. After all, she herself would never be the woman that Joshua could love. He'd made that very evident. He'd been trying to push her away from the moment they'd met.

"It turns out I believe in willpower, too," she declared. "With just a little bit of effort, you and I can resolve our differences. After all, neither one of us really wants to prolong our battle the rest of the semester."

Joshua picked up a child's crayon drawing and studied it critically. "We've gotten off track. Right now we're only concerned with awarding prizes for this science fair."

"Okay, Dr. Williams, you get the grand prize—for pure obstinacy! You're capable of going through this entire day without making even one attempt to compromise. And maybe you'll go through the rest of your life like that. Never admitting that maybe *you've* had something to do with this mess we're in." Sara went on pacing the classroom, with its posters of sleepy bears, studious turtles and playful kangaroos. Too bad there wasn't a poster of a mule in here, to represent Joshua Williams. But then he surprised her.

"Dammit, Sara, I know just how responsible I am for this mess. I'm not shrugging off any blame. I think about—" He stopped abruptly. "Never mind what I think about. But it's all the more reason for you and me to stop working together. Immediately."

Sara stood beside the blackboard and traced a finger through the yellow chalk dust. "We're getting somewhere. We've acknowledged that we're both part of the problem. That's a beginning."

"I want an end. Ms. Bennett, why can't you simply quit? Is it just the money? If that's the reason—when you take another assistantship, I'll make up the difference in salary out of my own pocket. Seems logical enough."

Sara felt cold, even though the room was stuffy and warm. "You want to get rid of me that badly?"

He picked up another drawing scribbled in crayon and studied it as if hoping to find the next Rembrandt. "It would be the best thing for both of us if you left."

"No," she burst out. "It would be the best thing for *you*. I make you face emotions you'd rather not see, emotions that remind you too much of your family. And you'll do anything to kill those feelings, even if it means paying me off. Except that I won't let you pay me off, Dr. Williams. I need the money, all right, but I'll earn it properly. You're stuck with me until graduation!" She took a deep breath, then went on a little more calmly.

"Here's the deal. Between now and December, I'll make darn sure you and I don't have any

more . . . incidents. We'll only talk about work, and
we'll only talk about *that* when it's absolutely necessary. Plus, I'm going to drop all motions and grievances and countergrievances against you. I'm proving
that I can compromise. I don't see why you can't
compromise a little, too.''

Joshua remained silent for a long moment, standing there behind the teacher's desk as if it were a bar-
ricade. And Sara understood something else about
him. Teaching was a way for Joshua to be with people, to share with them, yet it also allowed him to
maintain a distance. And maintaining a distance
seemed to be more important to him than anything . . . especially where Sara was concerned. Well, she
wanted distance, too. She stuffed her hands into the
pockets of her jacket, waiting for his answer. At last
he nodded.

"You've made a fair offer, Ms. Bennett. I'm going
to accept it. For my part of the bargain, I'll drop that
Form B-29 and all the rest of the damn forms that
came afterward. And I'll take responsibility myself for
avoiding . . . all unnecessary contact between us.''

Sara curled her fingers inside her pockets. "So we
can return to the dean with a workable solution.''

"That's what it looks like.''

"Good.''

They stood awkwardly for another moment, not
looking at each other, and then Joshua sat down again
at the desk.

"We have a bunch of anxious kids out there in the
gym,'' he said. "We'd better decide on the winners.''

Sara sank back down into one of the little chairs.
She opened her notepad. "I vote to put the mouse-

trap in first place," she said in a businesslike voice. "I still hate to choose winners, but since I'm forced into it, I vote for the mousetrap."

"I'll agree on that one. For second place, I'm debating between the cookie machine and the automatic dishwasher."

Sara stared at Joshua. His hair was rumpled and the collar of his plaid shirt was twisted awry—as if he'd just come through a tornado on the Colorado plains instead of merely arguing with Sara. But he looked grim and determined to be businesslike himself. Their bargain had already begun. For the rest of the semester, they would cooperate in a cool, professional manner—no heated emotions allowed. Yet all the cool cooperation in the world couldn't change one fact: Sara was more afraid than ever that she might fall in love with Joshua.

SARA WALKED SLOWLY through the conservatory, surrounded by lush greenery and air so humid it was heavy against her skin. She passed by the scarlet stars, the emerald ferns, the blood orange and the black bamboo. Her graduation gown floated around her legs and the tassel of her mortarboard dangled in her face. She pushed back the tassel, kneeling in front of her favorite plant—the heart of fire. She ran her fingers over its long, slender leaves. Today the plant seemed a little droopy to her, even melancholic, reminding her of fireworks that had fizzled out before they'd even begun.

"Goodbye," Sara murmured to the heart of fire and to all the plants. It had finally arrived, the day she'd been waiting for. Graduation. She knew she ought to be happy and excited about her future. Instead she felt as gloomy as the heart of fire drooping in front of her. Blast it, what was wrong with her? She wanted to be happy!

"I see you're communing with the plants again, Ms. Bennett," Joshua remarked from the end of the path. "Somehow I thought I'd find you in here, doing just that."

Sara straightened up. She glanced around at the lipstick tree, the coconut palms, the pepper vine. "I'm going to miss this place. I hope you'll take good care of the plants, especially my giraffe plant."

"I'll do my best as a botanist," Joshua said dryly.

"That's not enough. The heart of fire needs extra affection right now. Can you give the plants affection?"

One of those sour looks came over Joshua's face. "Ms. Bennett, you can trust me to handle things here."

It wasn't easy for Sara, relinquishing a responsibility that had come to mean so much to her. She felt at home in this conservatory. All semester, whenever Joshua had aggravated her the most, she'd been able to come here and soothe herself, digging her fingers into moist soil, pruning and feeding and misting the plants. She and Joshua had even shared some companionable moments here, times when they'd been able to forget their differences for a little while, at least. But those times were over. Sara had to leave. She walked quickly up the path, hoping that Joshua would move aside so she could go—and get on with her life. Instead of moving, however, he held out a yellow slicker to her.

"You left this at my house... the night of the banquet. I thought you'd want it back."

"Yes, of course. And that reminds me." Sara scrunched up her graduation gown so she could reach into the pocket of her skirt. She took out Joshua's ghastly purple tie and handed it over in exchange for her slicker.

"Seems like a fair trade," she said, holding the slicker next to her. "But if you'll take my advice— don't ever wear that tie again."

He smoothed the awful purple thing out on the palm of his hand and frowned at it in puzzlement. "I always liked this tie before you came along, Ms. Bennett. Now...I just don't know." Sara gazed at the tie, too, knowing that Joshua's purple ties and mismatched socks would no longer be a part of her life. She would no longer see his vivid color every day....

"Well, goodbye," she said in a rigid voice. "The graduation ceremony will begin any minute now. I have to get out of here."

Still he didn't move; he continued blocking the path. "I hear that you got straight A's this semester."

She stared at the rough texture of his corduroy jacket. "That's right."

He cleared his throat. "Not bad. Not bad at all."

"I'll assume you're giving me a compliment. Careful, Dr. Williams. You're getting almost effusive these days."

"Dammit, Sara—" He stopped himself, looking more and more out of sorts. After a moment he went on. "I suppose you've already completed your application to the Farm Managers Program."

"Yesterday I sent them the last piece of paperwork they needed—my grade transcript. But you still think I'm a hopeless dreamer about my farm, don't you?"

"I hate to see you heading for some big disappointment, that's all. The Farm Managers can't solve all your problems. You need something more—"

"Thanks for your concern, Joshua."

"Dammit, I *am* concerned about what happens to you. But that's something you won't believe."

"I don't know what to believe," she said quietly. "Except that you're relieved to be getting rid of me. That's the one thing I know for sure. And, deep down, I'm relieved to be going. These last four months— we've just about driven each other crazy."

"I'll agree with you there," Joshua said.

"So we finally agree on something."

They stared at each other. A tension seemed to permeate the heavy air, as if all the plants were bending forward, listening carefully to hear whatever would be said next. Sara felt as if she were surrounded by silent eavesdroppers. She could imagine how Joshua would scoff at *that* fancy.

"The thing is, you and I simply don't get along," she declared. "We truly are incompatible, just as you've been saying. If we tried another sort of relationship...it wouldn't work out, you know. I need someone who can share my dreams for the farm. And you need someone who won't ask you to 'emote' all the time."

"You have it all figured out, don't you, Sara?"

"Well, yes—"

"You don't actually want someone to share the farm with you. That would threaten your self-sufficiency. You *like* being self-sufficient, guarding your parents' memory all on your own. You're damn stubborn and unwilling to admit you need anybody's help. Lord, and then you complain about me.''

Sara tightened her fingers on her rain slicker. ''I could share my farm...with the right person. But maybe it's better to be self-sufficient. I'm proud of being that way. I'm not going to change anytime soon. Just like you're not going to change. You'll go on keeping all your emotions bottled up inside. You won't share them with me or with anyone else. You'll probably end up rattling around this conservatory all on your own.''

''And you'll rattle around that farm on your own.''

''I imagine we'll both be very happy. Alone and happy.''

''I like being alone, Sara.''

''So do I.''

''You'll have all your goats with the flower names.''

''You'll have Laddie.''

They were silent for a long moment. Then Joshua stirred.

''Listen, Sara,'' he said in a gruff voice. ''In spite of everything—I wish you luck.''

''You, too, Joshua. Good luck.''

They stared at each other again and Sara told herself this was the last time she'd ever see him. It was for the best, of course. She knew that, yet an ache was growing inside her. And in spite of her better judgment, she wished Joshua would stop her from leaving. She longed for that. If he'd stop her, she wouldn't care about anything else. She'd go to him gladly and worry about all the rest of it later. If only he would reach out his arms to stop her...

But he didn't reach for her. Instead he stood aside on the path, his face giving away nothing—no sadness, no regret to see her go. His eyes were as dark as a stormy sky, but she could read nothing in them, either. Nothing.

Sara brushed past Joshua, tears stinging her own eyes. And at last she fled the conservatory.

CHAPTER TWELVE

SARA SAT IN THE CREAKY old swing on her front porch, rocking back and forth. Years ago Grandpa Bennett had wanted to do away with the swing; he'd felt it didn't go with the Grecian pillars and ornate balustrades he had planned for the porch. But Sara's father, a young boy at the time, had convinced Grandpa Bennett to keep it. Sara's front porch therefore reflected an odd combination of quaint country farmhouse and grandiose country estate. But she liked it that way; she cherished the hodgepodge of her own heritage. She had wonderful plans to renovate the rest of her farm, but she wanted to keep all the family memories of her house intact.

The air was warm for a winter afternoon and Sara stretched her legs luxuriously until the toes of her buckaroo boots were heated by the sun. She turned a page of her book on flowers and gazed speculatively at a photograph of mountain candytuft blooms. Candytuft...hmm, she wasn't too sure about the sound of that.

A shiny blue Jeep came along the road to Sara's farm and stopped right in front of her house. Joshua Williams swung down from the vehicle, followed a few seconds later by his elderly collie. Laddie wagged his long, plumed tail and hobbled up the porch steps to greet Sara.

Her heart seemed to be thudding in her throat. She hadn't seen Joshua in almost two months...ever since that day in the conservatory. Blast him, what was he doing here now? She'd finally started to get a little of her equilibrium back. The last thing she needed was a visit from the almighty Dr. Joshua Williams!

Sara leaned down to pet Laddie. She was glad to see the collie, but the dog's master was another thing entirely. She gazed coolly at Joshua. His russet hair was rumpled, as if he'd been running his hands through it. He wore a plaid shirt in vivid red, green and blue, with navy corduroy trousers. He was also wearing hiking boots and Sara couldn't tell if his socks matched today. Darn, he looked good, but she wouldn't let on that she thought so.

"Hello, Dr. Williams. What brings you out here?"

"Hello...Sara." Joshua looked her over with a grave expression. He didn't say anything more, just went on looking at her for a long moment. Sara shifted in the swing, making it creak vociferously. And still Joshua just stood there and gazed at her. Sara tapped her heels on the porch.

"Joshua, *did* you come out here for a particular reason?"

The blasted man went right on staring at her in perplexed concentration. But at last he spoke. "Heard you were accepted by the Farm Managers. Thought I'd stop by and—congratulate you."

Sara had learned only yesterday that she'd been accepted into the program. She'd been elated, yet at the same time she wished she could share her elation.

Somehow Joshua had been the first person she'd thought of when she'd heard the good news. But could she share anything with a man who refused to acknowledge his emotions? And did he want to share anything with her?

"I'm surprised to hear you congratulating me," she said slowly. "All along you've been telling me that I've put too much hope in the program. All along you've been telling me that I'm a dreamer."

He looked disgruntled. "I never wanted you to fail. I just didn't want to see you get disappointed, that's all. And I knew you deserved to be in the program or I wouldn't have had the dean write that letter—" He stopped himself abruptly. Sara sat up straighter in the swing.

"What letter, Joshua? What are you talking about?"

"It's no big deal," he said gruffly. "I told Dean Logan you'd been...a decent research assistant. Maybe even more than decent, and that he ought to write a letter of recommendation for you. So that's what he did. He wrote a recommendation for you and sent it off to the head of the Farm Managers Program."

"You had him do that—for me?" Sara grinned. And Joshua looked even more disgruntled.

"Like I told you, it was no big deal. You probably would've been accepted whether or not anybody wrote a letter."

Suddenly Sara felt very happy. She rocked back and forth in the swing, pushing herself with the heels of her boots. "Maybe you believe in my dreams a little, af-

ter all. And maybe you're just as softhearted as mush,
although you'll never admit it.''

Joshua scowled at her. "Maybe I gave the dean an
accurate description of your abilities. Nothing more,
nothing less.''

"You're softhearted, all right, Dr. Williams. Laddie knows it. I know it. There's no escaping the fact.''

Joshua made a very obvious and very determined
effort to change the conversation. "I expected to find
you in the middle of some big job. Already breaking
ground for your dairy or trying out new machinery.
Something like that.''

"Oh, I'm in the middle of a big job, all right." She
gestured at her book. "I'm trying to decide on names
for all the new goats I'll have around here. So far I've
decided on Zinnia, Marigold and Columbine. I'm not
sure about Candytuft, though. I just can't picture
calling a goat Candytuft.''

Joshua's mouth twitched, and Sara looked at him
suspiciously.

"Was that a smile?" she demanded.

He arranged his features into a severe expression
again. Then he came up the porch steps and leaned
against one of Grandpa Bennett's Grecian pillars.
"Sara, I have something to say to you and I might as
well get on with it." Only he didn't get on with anything. He simply leaned there against the pillar, looking cranky and uncomfortable.

"Go ahead," Sara urged. She patted Laddie's head,
waiting. And at last Joshua spoke again.

"All right, this is it. What I want to say is—I've
come to a realization. I've realized that you and
I... dammit, that you and I might not be so incom-

patible, after all. In fact, I think we may even be . . . compatible.''

Sara stopped rocking in the swing. She gazed up at him. ''Compatible—that's a pretty strong word coming from you, Joshua.''

''Hear me out,'' he muttered. ''It's logical, when you put all the facts together and analyze them. Number one, you and I are both stubborn, Sara. Not just me—both of us. Neither one of us wants to accept our weaknesses, our limitations, whatever you want to call them. And that means when we take something on, we're likely to stick with it all the way. That's good, it's very good. Especially if we were to undertake a partnership together. We'd have an excellent chance of making it work, just out of sheer stubbornness. Number two—''

''I think we ought to discuss item number one a little more thoroughly.'' Sara's heart was really thumping now, but she made herself sound as scientific and analytical as Joshua. ''You mentioned the word 'partnership' in there somewhere. Let's clarify that. What exactly made you come to the realization that you and I could be partners?'' It was an unromantic word, quite matter-of-fact, but Sara found she liked the sound of it. Partners . . .

Joshua ran a hand through his hair, rumpling it still further. ''You're not making things easy. But this is how it happened. They sent a new research assistant over to me this semester. I hired her right on the spot. I didn't even mind that she was pretty—damn pretty, in fact. And that was when I knew I was in big trouble.''

''Just how pretty is this girl?''

"You're missing my point," Joshua said. "The first time I saw *you*, Sara—Lord, your hair was in that braid and I wanted to start undoing the braid right away...." He coughed, making an unsuccessful attempt to appear scientific again. "What I'm trying to say is... dammit, you affected me from the very beginning. I knew if I felt that way about you the very first day, we were in for one hell of a semester. That's why I tried so hard to get rid of you. I didn't want to be affected. But hiring this new research assistant didn't bother me at all. Still doesn't bother me. I'll never file Form B-29 to get rid of her."

"Joshua, is this supposed to make me feel good or something?" Sara rocked a little more. The swing gave a bewildered screak.

"I don't know how it's supposed to make you feel," he grumbled. "But this is how it is. My new assistant doesn't get under my skin. Never will. And that's what made me realize the truth. You're the one under my skin, Sara. You and no one else." Joshua delivered this pronouncement in an accusing tone, as if Sara were like a burr that had worked its way into his shoe. Sara didn't mind; she didn't mind at all. Her happiness was growing, strong and deep, but she maintained a serious demeanor.

"A partnership is the only solution," Joshua went on in a businesslike fashion. "Item number two— turns out we need each other, Sara. You need me on this farm, no matter how self-sufficient you'd like to be. The Farm Managers can't be your whole answer. You need my help and somehow I'll convince you of that."

"Maybe I have been too self-sufficient," she answered soberly. She meant to be as businesslike as he was, but Joshua had the strangest effect on her: his gruff manner only seemed to encourage her own emotions. "Oh, Joshua... I was so lonely after my parents died and you made me feel the loneliness worse than ever. That scared the heck out of me. Because it meant there was a place in my life only you could fill. Darn it, ever since you helped me bring in the harvest, you've belonged on this farm right along with me. I tried to fight that. I tried telling myself I didn't need you—but you're here now and I don't ever want you to leave again. And if you could share my dreams for the farm, just a little, I believe we really could have a partnership. I'm certainly willing to consider it, anyway."

He hooked his thumbs into the pockets of his corduroys and gazed out over the stubbled cornfields. "I want you to teach me about your dreams," he said in a low voice. "The flower-goat dairy and all the rest. Except I'll always see the practical side of things. I can't change that—"

"We'll have practical dreams together, too. Those are the very best kind, when you think about it."

"It's a deal then," he said with a relieved air. "We can embark on a partnership."

Sara left the swing and went to stand in front of him. "Listen," she began. "I'm glad we're not going to ask each other to change. That's a very sound basis for a partnership—accepting each other, and all. I mean, I'll never ask you to get histrionic like your family. I know what you're like inside and that's more than enough for me. But if you could just tell me one thing—"

He studied her gravely. "Did I mention item number three yet? Number three... I love you, Sara."

Joy swept through her, fresh as the wind over the Colorado plains. "I love you, too, Joshua."

Now his arms were around her, holding her close. "Sara, Sara..." His voice was husky, transforming her name into an endearment, a benediction. He kissed her, his lips warm and passionate on hers. There was so much passion inside Joshua. He had a heart of fire. Sara smiled. She wrapped her arms around his neck and held him fiercely.

"Yes," she murmured. "Yes, I accept your proposal for a partnership. I accept it wholeheartedly. But I have a few items of my own to discuss. Number four, after we're married I want you to hang up all your art posters in this house—our house. We'll have so many memories of our own to start building here."

"Okay, I'll agree to that, but here's item number five. None of our children will ever have to tap-dance unless it's exactly what they want to do."

Laddie wagged his tail to approve this item and Sara nodded her own agreement. She twined her fingers in Joshua's unruly red hair and grinned at him. "This partnership of ours is getting pretty complicated. To keep it all straight, maybe we'd better file Form 293-A, Motion to Unite Contrary Botanists and Fractious Research Assistants."

"In quadruplicate," Joshua murmured. And then he drew her close and kissed her again, telling her without any words this time just how very much he loved her.

HARLEQUIN ROMANCE®

**Harlequin Romance
knows that lasting love
is something special . . .**

And so is
next month's
title in

THE BRIDAL COLLECTION

TEMPORARY ARRANGEMENT
by Shannon Waverly

THE BRIDE was an unwelcome guest.
THE GROOM was a reluctant host.
The arrangement was *supposed*
to be temporary but—
THE WEDDING made it for keeps!

Available this month in
The Bridal Collection
RESCUED BY LOVE
by Anne Marie Duquette #3253

Wherever Harlequin books are sold.

Where do you find hot Texas nights, smooth Texas charm and dangerously sexy cowboys?

COWBOYS AND CABERNET

Raise a glass—Texas style!

Tyler McKinney is out to prove a Texas ranch is the perfect place for a vineyard. Vintner Ruth Holden thinks Tyler is too stubborn, too impatient, too... Texas. And far too difficult to resist!

CRYSTAL CREEK reverberates with the exciting rhythm of Texas. Each story features the rugged individuals who live and love in the Lone Star State. And each one ends with the same invitation...

Y'ALL COME BACK... REAL SOON!

Don't miss **COWBOYS AND CABERNET** by Margot Dalton. Available in April wherever Harlequin books are sold.

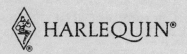